A CRAZY MIXED-UP SPANGLISH DAY

GET READY FOR MORE GaBí!

GET READY FOR GABí!

A CRAZY MIXED-UP SPANGLISH DAY

by Marisa Montes

illustrated by Joe Cepeda

> ✳ That's Gabí. Not Gabi. As in Ga-BEE.
> With an accent. But not yet. And you're
> about to find out why!

SCHOLASTIC PRESS ✳ NEW YORK

Library of Congress Cataloging-in-Publication Data
Montes, Marisa.
A crazy mixed-up Spanglish day / Marisa Montes;
illustrated by Joe Cepeda.
p.   cm. — (Get ready for Gabi : 1)
"A Little Apple paperback."
Summary: In Northern California, Maritza Gabriela Morales Mercado
struggles to deal with the third-grade bully, to control her temper, and to
remember to speak Spanish at home and English at school.
ISBN 0-439-51710-9
[1. Schools — Fiction. 2. Bullies — Fiction. 3. Spanish language — Fiction. 4.
Puerto Ricans — United States — Fiction. 5. Family life — California —
Fiction. 6. California — Fiction.] I. Cepeda, Joe, ill. II. Title.
PZ7.M76365 Cr 2003
[Fic] — dc21   2002036564
10 9 8 7 6 5 4 3 2 1   03 04 05 06 07

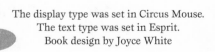

In loving memory of
my dear cousin "Miguelito"
Miguel Antonio Aponte Montes
July 22, 1947 – April 2, 2001
— M.M.

For Adriene
— J.C.

Acknowledgments

Special thanks to the third-grade teachers of Contra Costa Christian Schools in Walnut Creek, California, Sarah Gunst and Brian Huseland, for your time and patience. For all your insightful input, support, and encouragement, I'd like to thank Raquel Victoria Rodríguez, Susan Elya, Corrine Hawkins, Angie Williams. To third graders Ethan Williams and Janine Elya — you won't believe this! — a special BIG thanks for adding yet another dimension to Gabí.

Thanks to my family: Dr. Carmin Montes Cumming, my aunt, for being my Spanish consultant and being so enthusiastic about this project; my parents, Rubén and Mary Montes, for your constant love and belief in me; and my husband, David Plotkin, for all your love and support and computer expertise.

Thank you to my editor, Maria S. Barbo, for your wonderful ideas and suggestions, for brainstorming with me, and for your patience and flexibility in allowing me to write this book in my own style! And thanks especially to my agent, Barbara Kouts, for being a good friend and helping me be in the right place at the right time. Here's to good karma! — M.M.

CONTENTS

UNO
CHAPTER 1
BOOT TROUBLE!

"Expecting trouble?" Mr. Fine's bushy eyebrows knitted into one long, fuzzy caterpillar.

He eyed my red cowgirl boots.

Red. My favorite color.

Papi says red is bold and sassy, like me.

Mami says I'm *un ají picante* — a hot chili pepper — which is also red.

And in case you were wondering, I'm Maritza Gabriela Morales Mercado.

At home, I'm Gabi. At school, I'm Maritza Morales. Mercado is Mami's last name, so I don't use it in school.

"Maritza? The boots?" Mr. Fine waited for an answer.

"Well . . ." I sat up straight. "I thought there may be some . . . problems today."

I craned my neck to glare at Johnny Wiley. He sits a couple of rows to my left and one row back.

Johnny was spiking up his hair.

Today is Crazy-hair Day. Once a year, we get to wear our hair in weird, wacky ways. It's fun. Somehow Mami had gotten my wavy brown hair into two high ponytail braids — one over each ear.

You could tell Johnny thought he was soooo cool. His dark blond hair was all spiked and sprayed blue and red on the ends. Boys LOVE Crazy-hair Day. Most of them looked like wacko space monsters.

Johnny mouthed something. I knew what it was.

My eyes scrunched up.

He mouthed the words again. I made an I'll-get-you-later face.

"Maritza?"

My eyes snapped back to Mr. F. I flashed him my best good-girl smile.

Mr. F's long caterpillar eyebrow split back into two. They bounced high above his glasses.

"We've talked about this before, Maritza. There are better ways to solve . . . problems . . . than with one's feet."

My shoulders slumped. I nodded. "Yes, Mr. Fine."

Mr. F is the nicest teacher I've ever had. But sometimes, I don't think he remembers being a kid.

I looked up at Mr. Fine. He's tall and thin so he had to bend down to look at me eye to eye. "Don't make me have to tell you again, Maritza."

"But —"

"No buts. If you even aim one boot at another student, I'll take them away and I won't give them back to you until the end of the day."

I sank down at my desk and tucked my boots as far under my seat as they'd reach.

My favorite uncle, Tío Julio, sent me these boots. They have tiny stars and curly

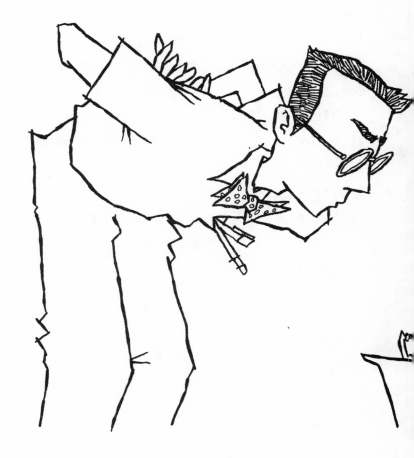

half-moons carved in the red leather and painted white.

Red and white: my favorite color combo.

Mr. Fine turned to the other students. "Okay, class. Take out a sheet of paper. As part of our new project, I want you to make a list of strange or interesting animals you'd like to learn about. Try not to choose common pets or farm animals."

Billy Wong asked, "What about Melvin?"

"Good question, Billy. An iguana is a very interesting animal."

Melvin is our class pet. Mr. F keeps him

in a big aquarium at the back of the room. We measured Melvin once. He's almost two feet long, if you count his striped tail.

There was a lot of mumbling. A few kids said, "Cool!"

I glanced at Johnny, moved one foot forward, and quietly tapped the toe of my boot.

I knew what I'd LIKE to write at the top of my list — the animal that looks most like Johnny Wiley: *Un sapo gigante* — a big, fat TOAD!

DOS
CHAPTER 2
"I HAVE THE FLY BEHIND MY EAR!"

Mr. Fine kept talking. He was walking slowly up and down the rows of desks.

"For this month's project, we'll break up the class into groups of three," Mr. Fine said. "Can anyone tell me how many groups that would be?"

Mr. F likes to check our math skills whenever he has a chance. Luckily, I like math. Numbers come easily to me.

What doesn't come easily is spelling. All those letters and rules! "I" before "e" or "e" before "i"? As Mami says, "*¡Ay, ay, ay, ay, ayyyyy!*"

7

I raised my hand.

So did one of my best friends, Jasmine Lange.

She had sprayed the tips of her black curls hot pink for Crazy-hair Day. Jasmine crossed her eyes at me.

I swallowed a giggle. I'm really lucky my teacher lets her sit right next to me.

"Jasmine?"

"Since there are eighteen students in our class, that would be six groups of three, Mr. Fine."

"That's right, Jasmine, six groups."

I crossed my fingers. "Do we get to choose who's in our group, Mr. Fine?"

Oops! I forgot to raise my hand. So, real quick, I stuck it up in the air.

"Not this time, Maritza." Mr. F waved a sheet of paper. "I've already made that decision."

Groans filled the room.

"Quiet down, class." He used his I-mean-it voice. "In real life, you won't always get to be in a group or a team with your best friends. You need to get used to what it's like to work with all sorts of people."

I started to get a bad feeling about this. I raised my hand again.

"Yes, Maritza?"

"Umm — Mr. Fine," I began. "I think I have the fly behind my ear."

The class broke into giggles.

Then Johnny said, "A fly? Sure! Flies love pizza! Maritza Pizza gets flies! Do you get fleas, too?"

He started to scratch under his arms like an itchy monkey.

"HEY!" I bolted toward Johnny.

Before I got two steps, Mr. Fine blocked

9

my path. His eyebrows knitted into that long, fuzzy caterpillar again.

He pointed to my seat.

I sat down.

Mr. Fine turned to Johnny. "John, that will be enough!"

My cheeks sizzled.

I clenched my teeth, crossed my arms over my chest, and stared straight ahead.

I felt like I'd bitten into some of Mami's raw *ajo* — garlic. Steam whooshed out of my ears.

"What's this about a fly, Maritza?" Mr. Fine peered behind my ears. "I don't see anything."

More giggles from the class. One glance from Mr. F and they shushed.

Now my whole face burned. "It's what Mami says when I have a feeling something bad is going to happen to me. She says I must have the fly behind my ear."

Mr. Fine nodded. Slowly. "Oh . . . I see . . . it's an idiom. From Puerto Rico?"

I shrugged. I wasn't sure what that meant.

Mr. F turned to write on the chalkboard.

Then — you won't believe this! — Johnny Wiley started hopping up and down the aisle, doing his itchy monkey act. He was all bent over and scratching under his arms.

"Maritza Pizza has flies!" He whispered so Mr. F couldn't hear. "Maritza Pizza has fleas!"

A few kids laughed.

I glared at Johnny. He gave me his nasty Wiley smile and sat down — real quick, before Mr. Fine could see him.

Billy Wong, one of Johnny's buddies, gave him a high five — but it was under the desk, so I guess it was a low five.

I turned around to look at my other best friend, Devin Suzuki. She sits right behind me. We were both wearing our hair almost the same way for Crazy-hair Day. We sprayed the braids purple. You couldn't really see it on my hair, but the purple was super-bright on Devin's because it's a lighter brown than mine.

Devin tugged her right braid and winked. Our secret it's-okay sign. We signal with our hair whenever we know the other one is feeling bad.

It made me feel better right away.

I tugged my right braid back at her and gave her a half grin.

On the chalkboard, Mr. F wrote the word IDIOM.

"An *ih-dee-um*," he pronounced the word slowly. "It's an expression — something people from a place or country say a lot and it catches on. Like 'The early bird catches the worm.'"

He turned to the class. "Can anyone give me another example of an idiom?"

Devin raised her hand. "That kid has ants in his pants?"

Then Devin glared at Johnny. Johnny just gave her a creepy Wiley smile.

Mr. F didn't notice. "Good, Devin. Anyone else?"

I grinned at Devin and gave my right braid a double tug. That means "Cool! Good job!"

Devin smiled so big I could see her braces. Devin has metal braces on her two front teeth to fill in the gap between them.

She must be happy because she doesn't usually smile big enough to show her braces. She's very shy about them.

She's very shy about *everything*. Basically, Devin's a very shy kid.

Sissy Huffer, NOT a good friend, raised her hand. "She's as mad as a wet hen?" Sissy was looking right at me when she said that.

I just stared, like I had no idea what she meant.

"That's right, Sissy. Very good." Mr. F nodded.

Sissy gave me a snooty smile and shook her blond curls. Sissy doesn't do anything for Crazy-hair Day. She can't stand to mess up her perfect curls.

"Apparently in Puerto Rico," Mr. F continued, "when someone has a feeling something bad is going to happen, people say — what's the expression, Maritza?"

"You have the fly behind your ear." I grinned. "Want to hear it in Spanish?"

"Please." Mr. Fine bowed. He gave me the go-ahead sign with a swish of his arm.

"*Tienes la mosca detrás de la oreja.*"

Mr. Fine knew a little Spanish. He wrote the phrase on the board.

"Maybe we can share idioms from other countries during the school year."

Back at his desk, he picked up the sheet of paper he had earlier.

"Now, for the six groups of three," he said. "Group One: Billy Wong, Mike Patel, and Jasmine Lange. Group Two: Sissy Huffer, Johnny Wiley, and Maritza Morales. Group Three . . ."

My eyes bugged out. I didn't hear the rest.

Johnny Wiley AND Sissy Huffer?

In the same group?

With me?

Working together?

¡Caracoles! Yikes! I KNEW I had the fly behind my ear!

CHAPTER 3
DOUBLE TROUBLE

"¡*Ay, ay, ay!*" Devin stopped so fast, I bumped right into her.

It was recess and we'd just stepped out of the girls' room. We were playing follow the leader on the way to the playground to meet Jasmine. She always races to the monkey bars the moment the doors open.

Devin was the leader today.

She skipped. I skipped.

She stuck out her rear and did a hip-wiggle dance. I stuck out my rear and did a hip-wiggle dance.

She hopped on one foot. I hopped on one foot.

She stopped short. I bumped right into her.

"*¿Qué?*" I glanced around. "What?"

"*¡Mira!*" Devin pointed. I looked.

Devin likes to practice her Spanish with me. Her family lived in Panama for four years while her dad worked for an American company there. She speaks really good Spanish, and she doesn't want to forget it.

"Isn't that your Little Buddy, Cecilia?" Devin asked.

Each third grader gets to be a Big Buddy to a kindergartner. We help them with special projects during school.

I got Cecilia Sanchez because she just moved to California from Nicaragua. She didn't speak much English yet.

Little Cecilia was squatting next to a tree by the kindergarten play area. She looked like a scared kitty. Cecilia's hands covered her face.

She was crying buckets of tears, or as Mami would say — *lloraba a lágrima viva.*

We ran to the play area.

"¿Qué pasa, Ceci?" I asked her what was wrong.

The moment Ceci saw me, she wrapped her arms around my middle. She stuck her face in my chest and cried harder.

I held her tight. Ceci is even smaller than I was at her age.

It made me feel very big. And important.

I wondered if that was what Papi felt like when he held me.

"Tell me, Ceci," I said in Spanish. *"Dime."*

She mumbled something into my chest.

"Ceci . . ." I pulled her away from me. Gently.

She grabbed back on and buried her face in my chest.

I tried once more. *"Dime, Ceci. ¿Qué pasa?* Tell me. What's wrong?"

But every time I pulled her away, she snapped back like a rubber band.

"Shh, *cálmate, cálmate* . . . calm down . . ." I whispered nice things to her. Like Mami does to me when I wake up crying from a nightmare.

"Is there a problem, girls?" Ms. Snippett, the teacher on duty, walked up to us.

"*No sé,*" I told her.

Ms. Snippett just stared, like she didn't get what I'd said.

Then I realized I was speaking Spanish to a non-Spanish-speaking teacher. I was so upset, I was crossing my brain wires.

My face turned the color of my boots.

There's only one thing I can't stand more than Johnny Wiley: And that's mixing up Spanish and English. I only do it when I'm super-stressed.

I'm *very* proud of how well I can speak both languages. And I don't like making mistakes. It's soooooo embarrassing!

I looked up. "I mean, I don't know."

"Why are you crying, dear?" Ms. Snippett asked Ceci.

I shook my head. *"No entiende —* I mean, she doesn't understand much *inglés —* uh, English."

"Oh. Well, ask her again. In Spanish."

So I did. *"¿Qué pasa, Ceci?"* I pulled her away so I could hear.

My T-shirt was all wet. From tears and . . . I tried not to think of what else. Ceci had goo running from her nose.

"Un muchacho malo . . ." Ceci said, really blubbering.

Ms. Snippett handed her a tissue to blow her nose. "What did she say?"

"Un muchacho malo . . ." I told her.

"Well, I heard *that,*" said Ms. Snippett. "But what does she *mean?*"

Uh-oh! My brain is really losing it, I thought. Devin gave me a worried smile.

"Something about 'a bad boy' . . ."

Before I could say anything else, Ms. Snippett took Ceci's hand. "Tell her I'm taking her to the office to get some water and to lie down."

"Okay . . ." I told Ceci what Ms. Snippett said. But I told her in English.

I sighed and told her again. This time in Spanish . . . *I hope.*

The moment Ms. Snippett took Ceci away, Johnny Wiley ran by.

After he passed us, he stopped and turned. With a big, nasty smirk, he waved. "Hey, Pizza Face! Hey, Metal Mouth!"

The moment he said "Metal Mouth," Devin's lips snapped over her braces. She looked ready to cry.

I bit my lip. My boots itched to kick him. I sprang forward.

Devin grabbed my arm. "No, Maritza, don't do it!"

"Hey, Pizza, catch any more flies

lately?" Johnny laughed. He could be soooo awful!

Billy Wong and a couple of Johnny's other buddies gathered around him.

Devin squeezed my arm harder and whispered warnings in Spanish.

Then Johnny spotted something behind us. His smirk widened.

Johnny nudged Billy and pointed. "Hey, there's that little crybaby again. She still blubbering?"

We turned.

You won't believe this! Johnny was pointing at Ceci.

I glared at him.

"That *sapo gigante*!" I said to Devin. "Now he's picking on little kids! Wait till I get him!"

"No, Maritza!" Devin cried. "You'll get detention . . . or worse. Remember what Mr. F said. He'll take away your boots!"

"I can't let him get away with that! I'd rather slurp slugs!"

I tried to pull away from Devin. But she wrapped both arms around me.

"Let go, Devin!"

Devin and I went back to yelling at each other in Spanish.

I tried to make her let go, but she wouldn't.

Johnny and his friends kept laughing.

Devin kept holding me.

My head was spinning.

"*¡Deja que te agarre!*" I yelled at Johnny.

"What's that?" he shouted back, grinning like a T-rex. "I don't speak-a the lingo, Pizza Face."

I felt like a bag of piping-hot microwave popcorn about to explode.

I did it again. I mixed up my Spanish and English.

And *this* time to Wiley the Smiley.

My toes curled in my boots.

Again I tried to yank away from Devin. But she stuck to me better than a sticker to a notebook.

I tried to drag her with me, but she was too heavy.

I stomped my boot. "Wait till I get you!" I yelled again.

This time in the right language . . . *I think.*

Johnny howled and punched the air with his fist. "Boys RULE, girls drool!"

He and Billy high-fived. Then they started hopping and scratching under their arms, all hunched over like itchy monkeys.

"Oh, yeah?" I yelled back. "Well . . . well . . . go chew monkey chow!"

CUATRO
CHAPTER 4
TROUBLE STRIKES AGAIN!

"Okay, class," Mr. Fine said once we'd all settled down after recess. "As I started to explain this morning, for this month's project we're going to work together in teams. Each team will choose a different animal to study. Remember, the animal should be strange or interesting."

Our desks were already pushed together into our new teams.

I'd never seen six groups of grumpier third-grade faces. Papi would call them *caras largas* — long faces. That's what they say in Argentina, where he's from. Mami would say they had faces as long as a *güiro*.

A *güiro* is a musical instrument. It's made from a long gourd that's dried and hollowed out. Then they carve slashes on the sides. You play it by scraping the slashes with a metal fork. It makes a *grrr-grrr, grrr-grrr* sound like my little brother when he needs a nap.

I think *güiros* are fun.

Working in teams with your worst enemies is NOT fun.

And Mr. Fine had a talent for grouping people with their worst enemies.

On the other hand, Mr. F looked *más contento que un perro con dos rabos* — happier than a dog with two tails.

Mr. Fine walked to

the board. He began to write as he spoke. "First, you'll work together to choose one or two animals from each team member's list — the lists you made this morning. Then you'll vote on which animal to use for your project.

"Finally, you'll present your animal to the class — as a *team*." He said the last word like he meant business. "You may write a report, perform a play, make a video, build a model, or do anything else the team chooses.

"All right. Go to it."

Everyone was quiet as we studied our own

lists. Finally, people started talking about what to write on the team's animal list.

Sissy wrinkled her nose. "Making lists reminds me of my mom's grocery lists, which reminds me of food. And thinking of food makes me hungry. I wish I had a snack."

"I know how you can get a snack, Sissy." Johnny gave me a wicked grin.

I pursed my lips, steeling myself for one of his nasty comments.

"How?" Sissy just HAD to ask.

"We have free food, right here in our own team," he said. "Just pick pepperoni and cheese right off Maritza Pizza!"

Billy Wong was sitting in the group next to us. He reached over and jabbed Johnny. "Free food from Maritza Pizza! Good one, Wiley!"

Johnny snickered, all happy with himself. "Hey, Maritza P—"

That did it! Before Johnny even finished the word, I was at his side.

I towered over him.

In my boots, I always feel as if I can tower over anybody. Even though I'm the smallest kid in the class.

I took my favorite position: fists on my hips, boots slightly apart, toes pointed out.

I stared at him. Hard. If I were Dragon-Ella with her laser gaze, Johnny would be crispy toast. But I'm Maritza Gabriela Morales Mercado and

my secret weapon is my good old pair of red boots.

I stomped my right boot once.

Johnny's eyes opened wide. He leaned away from me.

Twice.

Johnny let out a tiny squeak.

I grinned. *He won't be calling me THAT again for a long, long time. I promise you.*

"This one's for my Little Buddy, Ceci!" I growled.

Just as I hauled back my boot to kick him in the shin, I heard Mr. Fine call my name.

I could tell from his voice that I just went from Guate-*mala* to Guate-*peor*.

That means from *bad* to *worse*.

Then, the next thing I knew, Mr. F was making me take off my boots.

I spent the rest of the day walking around in my white socks!

CINCO
CHAPTER 5
"I'D RATHER EAT BEES!"

After school that day, I stomped into my bedroom and kicked off my boots. One boot went flying onto the bed. The other one almost banged me on the head. I grabbed them and hid them deep in my closet.

I ripped off my grubby socks and stuffed them in the laundry basket. Way down, under other clothes. There, Mami wouldn't notice how filthy they were until she did the laundry.

By then, she'd probably know what happened, anyway.

When I turned around, I felt like the walls were staring at me.

Actually, they were.

My walls are covered with posters. Some are of my favorite superheroes. Others are of real-life heroines I read about in a book called *Brave Women in History* that Abuelita, my grandmother, sent me from Puerto Rico. Mami and I read one story every night until we finished it.

Annie Oakley stared out from an old poster. She posed next to her saddle after a performance in *Buffalo Bill's Wild West Show.* She was NOT smiling.

Even Iviahoca, my favorite Taino heroine, didn't look happy. You say her name like this: ee-veeyah-HOH-kah. "Taino" is tah-EE-noh. The Taino were the natives who lived in Puerto Rico and nearby islands when Christopher Columbus landed.

Mami told me that Iviahoca means "behold the mountain that reigns" in the Taino language. Iviahoca was a very brave woman. She even risked her life to save her son when he was captured by Spanish soldiers.

I couldn't find a big picture of Iviahoca, so last summer, I drew her with crayons on poster paper. She's standing on a cliff, watching Spanish ships sail into a bay in Puerto Rico.

On the same wall, the Latin-American superwoman Dragon-Ella frowned down at me from a huge poster. A dark green cape — like dragon wings — blew behind her. With her jaws clenched, fists on hips, legs apart (my favorite pose), she can take on anything.

When I was a little kid, I used to think I could grow up to be a superhero like Dragon-Ella. I thought that if I wished long enough and worked hard enough, I could get superpowers like hers.

Of course, I couldn't. Superheroes only

exist in the movies or on TV or in the comics. But I never gave up on wanting to fight crime.

Someday, I'm going to grow up to be the head of a secret government agency. And the president of the United States will call me on a special red phone.

I'll live a double life: Everyone will think I'm a karate and kick-boxing teacher. But I'll really be fighting crime under a secret identity.

I plopped onto the bed and looked at my walls. All my favorite heroines stared down at me.

I held out my hands.

"Well, what did you want me to do?" I asked them. "I couldn't let him get away with it!"

Thinking I was talking to him, Tippy, my black-and-white tomcat, jumped onto my bed. (My family says his name the Spanish way — TEE-pee. I like to pick names for my pets and toys that are easy to say in both languages.)

Tippy greeted me in his usual way.

First, he rubbed up against my leg, sweet as could be.

Next, he stomped over my bare feet.

It's such a silly thing to do, I always have to laugh — even on a yucky day like today.

"Come on, Tippy!" I scooped him up and swished him around. "You want to fly like Dragon-Ella?"

I landed Tippy on the bed next to me.

"You won't believe this, Tippy! Mr. Fine *me quitó las botas* — he took away my boots. He said I wasn't allowed to wear them to school ever again."

I always talk to Tippy in Spanish. That's all he speaks. Not like me or my family. We speak English *and* Span-ish. But at home, we *only* speak Spanish.

That's why Tippy doesn't understand anything else.

"I spent the afternoon walking around school in my socks. Mr. F only gave them back to me so I could walk home."

Tippy looked at me and slowly closed his big green eyes. Then he turned his head away. He couldn't be more bored.

"Tippy!" I wiggled the mattress to get his attention.

Tippy's eyes flew open. But when he saw it was just me, he closed them again.

I sat up and tickled my silly cat behind the ears. *"Esto es serio,* Tippy. This is serious! Mr. Fine made me promise never to wear my boots to school again. And to make sure I won't forget, he wrote it in a note to Mami and Papi.

"They have to

sign the note, and I have to bring it back to school tomorrow. *¡Caracoles!*" I flopped back on the bed.

Tippy stretched and yawned. Then he lay on his side and got comfortable.

This time I had to smile.

I couldn't help it. I just remembered the look on Johnny's face.

"You know what, Tipito?" (Tipito means "Little Tippy.") "The look on Johnny Wiley's face and that little squeak he made when he thought I was going to kick him made it all worth it."

Tippy started purring. His eyes were closed. His lips curled up in a kitty smile. The black spot on his chin wiggled like he was laughing.

"*Miaouu . . .*" he said softly.

"I knew you'd understand!" I hopped up so I was standing on the mattress. "You wouldn't have let old Wiley the Smiley get away with that nasty comment, either, would you, Tipito? Well, I didn't."

I started jumping on the bed.

"Nope!" I jumped. "*¡Claro que no!* No way!" I jumped higher. "I'd rather eat bees!"

I jumped so high and so hard, Tippy went flying. He landed on my rug and flicked his tail at me in a huff.

Then I noticed the heroines on my walls. They didn't seem as grumpy now.

"Come on, Tipito." I hopped off the bed and picked him up.

He squirmed a little. Then he licked my nose with his warm, sandpaper tongue.

I giggled. "Now, to make sure Mami and Papi don't take away my boots, too."

SEIS
CHAPTER 6
"WHEN THE FROG
GROWS HAIR!"

"Gabi! Gabi! Gabi!"

A few minutes later, Miguelito, my four-year-old brother, came bouncing into my room. He just figured out I was home.

Like my parents, Miguelito always calls me by my middle name. When I was little, I couldn't say "Maritza Gabriela." But I could say "Gabi," short for "Gabriela." So Mami and Papi started calling me Gabi, too.

I was lying on my bed again. I groaned and rolled over.

Maybe he'll think I'm asleep . . .

"Gabi!" He yelled in my ear. His voice was as loud as a car horn.

. . . *Or maybe not.*

My ear was ringing. I grabbed my pillow and covered my head.

Miguelito was still yelling and bouncing next to me.

I dragged the pillow from my face.

"*Cuchichea,*" I told him softly. "If you want to get someone's attention, whisper, okay?"

Mami did this to me when I was little, and it worked. It's amazing! She always made me listen by just speaking softly.

Maybe it would work with Miguelito . . .

He leaned over and whispered in my ear. "Gabi, guess what?"

"What?" I whispered back.

"MAMI AND PAPI HAVE A SECRET!"

. . . *Or maybe not.*

I grinned. If anybody stops talking when

Miguelito walks in on them, he thinks they have a secret.

Miguelito likes to blab everything he hears, so Mami and Papi don't talk about grown-up stuff when he's around. The moment he bounces into the room, they change the subject or stop talking.

But . . . you never know . . .

I sat up, ready to hear his big "secret."

"*¿De veras?*" I tried whispering again. "Really? How do you know?"

"Because they said something about —" He stopped.

I waited. His lips were pressed together. His eyes were as big as *platos* — plates. He was turning purple.

"*¡Respira!*" I said, giving his shoulder a little shake. "Breathe!"

Miguelito let out a big breath. He leaned in close. "*¡Una sorpresa!*" he whispered in my ear.

"A surprise?" I jumped up. Now *this* was something. "Are you sure?"

He nodded so hard his teeth rattled. And his dark hair flopped up and down.

"A surprise . . ." I repeated. "Hmm . . . Maybe I can snoop around after dinner."

"Can I snoop, too?" Miguelito started bouncing on his toes, letting his arms hang loose and limp. He looked like a floppy rubber doll on a string.

If I didn't answer soon, he'd let his jaw go all loosey-goosey. Then he'd moan, "Ahh-hhhhh," while he bounced and jiggled. So it would sound all jittery and jerky. He loved to do that.

He's such a goofball . . . but so am I!

I joined him, and we both bounced and jiggled and went, "Ahh-hhhh-hhh!"

"Soo-oo-oo, caa-aan III-eee snoo-ooop, too-oo?" he asked.

"Ooh-kaaaa-aaay," I answered.

Then I stopped and pressed a finger against my lips.

"But only if you're very, very *quiet*," I whispered. "Shhh . . ."

"Shhhh . . ." he whispered back.

Oh yeah, he'll be quiet, all right . . .

¡Cuando la rana eche pelo! — as Mami says. When the frog grows hair!

SIETE
CHAPTER 7
SPUNKY FEET

Fifteen minutes later, Miguelito was still jumping around my room. I needed to study for my spelling test, but he was NOT being quiet the way he'd promised.

"Miguelito," I said, grinning, "you'll be quiet *cuando la rana eche pelo,* won't you?"

Miguelito nodded and laughed extra loud. "HA! A froggie with hair!"

"*Shhh* . . . Think about it, Miguelito. Where would it grow? Between his toes?" I wiggled my bare toes. "Hairy frog webs!"

"Hairy webs! That would tickle!" He rolled on the carpet and laughed and laughed.

45

"Here," I said. "Show me how a froggie hops."

He crouched down and started hopping like a frog.

"That's right," I said, guiding him to the door. "Hop out to the family room for a while."

Miguelito's dark hair flip-flopped as he hopped. He'd make a good hairy frog.

Right then, Papi peeked in. When he saw Miguelito frog-hopping, he got down and started hopping, too. Then I got down. Now we were three hopping frogs.

Papi pooped out first and fell back on the carpet. I lay down next to him.

Miguelito bounced off to watch TV.

"How was your day, Gabita?" Papi asked when we were alone. He likes to call me "Little Gabi."

Papi tugged one of my ponytail braids. Then he kissed the top of my head.

I groaned and dragged myself to my desk. "Pretty yucky."

Papi pulled up a stool and sat next to me.

He nodded. "I had a pretty yucky day, too. One of my experiments blew up on me."

I checked him over. "No kidding. You forgot to take off your icky lab coat again."

Papi looked down at his lab coat. He nodded sadly. *"Es verdad.* So I did."

I like to think of Papi as a mad scientist. But the truth is that he's more like an absent-minded professor — like the one in that Disney movie. When he's working, he forgets about everything else.

Papi put his arm around me. *"Dime, Gabita.* Tell me what was so terrible about your day?"

I sighed and pulled Mr. F's note from under my book. "I can explain. I really can."

I told him about the whole awful day. As I talked, Papi's long, sad face got longer and sadder. He reminded me of a sad-eyed hound dog with droopy cheeks.

¡Pobre Papi! I'd made him feel bad.

Slowly, I handed him the note.

"Now Mr. Fine won't let me wear my boots to school. Will you sign this so Mami doesn't have to see it?"

He read the note.

"You're going to have to tell her, Gabi."

"Why? We can tell her later —"

"No. Mr. Fine wants us both to sign," he said. "Anyway, we do not keep secrets from your *mami*."

I sighed. I was hoping that after a day or so, Papi would forget.

I gave it one more try. "But Mami gets so upset when I get in trouble!"

Papi shook his head sadly. "She worries about you. So do I. Gabita, you must try to control your spunky feet."

I giggled. "I have spunky feet?"

49

Papi nodded. He bit his lower lip, trying to look serious. "Afraid so."

But his green eyes were laughing.

"Oh, Papi," I said, already starting to feel better, "you're such a big silly."

"No, you're the silly." Papi faced me in his chair, ready to play the game we've been playing since I was little.

"No, *you're* the silly." I leaned in closer. *"Papi bobo."*

"No, *you're* the silly." Papi leaned in even closer. *"Gabita bobita."*

"No, you're the —"

"¡Topi!" And that's when Papi bumped my forehead with his. "I got you!"

"¡Ay, Papi!" I said, grinning really big. *"¡Cuánto te quiero!"*

"I love you very much, too, Gabita." Papi kissed my forehead.

"Now," he said, sitting back, "we have to talk about how to solve problems . . . *without* the use of spunky feet."

OCHO
CHAPTER 8
MY SECRET IDENTITY

Papi and I moved to my bed where he could sit next to me.

"Gabita, your *mami* and I worry about your temper." He put his arm around my shoulders.

"But, Papi," I said, "Johnny makes me see red."

"I thought you liked red."

"I like red, not *Johnny*!" I said his name with my upper lip curled up — the way I say *booger*.

"Anyway, my job is to fight evil. And

Johnny Wiley is one of the great evils of the universe!" I stared at Papi. "He's my worst enemy! The way El Bandido is Dragon-Ella's worst enemy."

I waited for Papi to act like a grown-up and tell me that I'm too young to have "a job."

He didn't.

Instead, he said, "I can understand that. You do your job the best way you know how. But part of having a job is learning new ways to do it better."

"It is?" I sat up straight. This sounded interesting.

"Oh, absolutely. People who are very good at their jobs are good because they keep trying to get even better. That's why they call what your *mami* does *'practicing* law.'"

Papi pulled me close. "Me, too. I have to

keep studying to become a better chemist."

I looked up. "But you're already so good!"

"We want to *stay* good. And we want to get *better.*"

I thought about that. It made sense.

"So what should I do to be a better crime fighter?"

Papi scratched his cheek. "Well . . . might I suggest using your head, not your feet?"

My shoulders slumped. "No feet? But . . . they're my secret weapon — like Dragon-Ella's laser eyes."

"Superheroes only use their secret weapons when they have to. Look" — Papi took my hand — "doesn't Dragon-Ella lead a double life? And doesn't she do everything she can to protect her secret identity?"

"*¡Pues claro!* Of course she does!" I said. "Dragon-Ella is a firefighter. She can't let anyone know about her secret powers!"

"Why not?"

I rolled my eyes. Grown-ups sure are clueless sometimes. "Because she has to blend in with everyone else. Then the villains will let down their guards and make a mistake. That's how she finds out who the real bad guys are."

Papi nodded. "What would happen if she used her superpowers when she was fighting fires?"

"Papi!" I couldn't believe he had to ask. "Her cover would be blown. Then she couldn't catch the villains in the act and spoil their evil plans."

Papi smiled.

"Oh," I said, feeling a little silly I didn't catch on sooner. "I get it. I have to stop using my secret weapon at school. And I can't let on about my crime-fighting identity. My cover is third-grade student."

Papi kissed my forehead. "And a very good cover it is. Could even fool me. And I know the truth."

"But you're the only one."
I winked. "Let's keep it
that way, okay?"

Papi smiled. "You've al-
ways dreamed of fighting
crime, Gabita. I'm so proud of
you for that. You're never too
young to start living your dream.
But remember, you'll have to start
learning to use this" — Papi tapped
my forehead — "instead of these."
He pointed to my bare feet. "And
you have to pretend you're a
regular kid."

"But we know different,
don't we, Papi?"

"That's right, super-*hija*.
We know different."

I grinned and gave Papi
a great-big, super-daughter hug.

NUEVE
CHAPTER 9
"BURGER/, ANYONE?"

"*Mami, pasa las* french fries, *por favor,*" I said to Mami at dinner that night.

Papi and I wanted Mami to be in a good mood when she heard about Mr. F's note. So he and I made dinner: hamburgers with our secret sauce, fries, and Mami's favorite avocado salad with lime-and-garlic dressing.

"Gabi, please don't mix your Spanish with English. If you want the fries, say it in Spanish." Mami is very strict about Miguelito and I speaking good Spanish at home.

Miguelito slurped his milk — real loud — and almost spilled it.

While Mami fussed with him, I thought for a minute. "Um . . . I think I forgot how to say 'french fries.'"

"See what happens when you get lazy and use the English word when there's a perfectly good Spanish word? You forget the correct Spanish word." Mami passed the fries, and at the same time she said, *"Papas fritas."*

"Oh," I said, "that's right. *Papas fritas.*"

The last thing I wanted right now was to get Mami mad at me.

I glanced at Papi. He winked.

I bit into my hamburger. "Ummm, *muy bueno*, Papi. Very yummy."

Miguelito swung his legs as he munched on his burger. *"¡Sí, Papi, muy bueno!* Um-ummm! Yummy!"

"Mami, how do you like your —?" I gulped, almost choking on my burger.

I just realized I didn't know how to say "hamburger" in Spanish.

57

"*¿Cómo?*" Mami said. "What?"

"Uh . . ." My brain was racing. "Ham" is "*jamón*" in Spanish, but what is "burger"?

"Uh . . ." I tried again. "How do you like your *jamón-burgera?*"

Papi really did choke on his burger. He laughed and laughed and laughed.

Even Mami chuckled. "I think you mean *hamburguesa,* Gabi. But that was a very good try!"

"Ummm!" said Miguelito. "*Jamón-burgera!*"

His legs swung happily under the table as he took another big bite.

This time, everyone laughed.

After dinner, Papi asked, "Anyone ready for dessert?"

"*YAAAY!*" Miguelito clapped and swung his legs.

I clapped, too.

Then Miguelito and I started banging our spoons on the table. "*¡Helado! ¡Helado! ¡Helado!*"

I knew Papi had made his special *helado de coco* — coconut ice cream. We all love it.

Papi's timing was perfect.

Mami had on her grumpy *güiro* face. During dinner, Papi had told her about Mr. F's note. She was *not* happy.

Neither was I. I had a *cara larga*, too. I wondered if Mr. F's note had spoiled their surprise — whatever it was.

So I hopped up, glad to have something

fun to do. "Let me help, Papi! I'll get the *helado* from the *friser* —"

I shot a look at Mami. Her eyebrows flew up under her light brown curls.

Friser is Spanglish for "freezer" or "fridge." Mami hates when I use Spanglish.

Spanglish is when you take an English word and add some Spanish to it. Or when you say an English word with a Spanish accent, like *friser*. It sounds like it's really Spanish, but it's not.

"I mean *congelador,*" I said.

"Maybe we should save it," Mami said. "Until after . . ." She gave Papi a funny look.

"Until after what, Mami?" Miguelito wiggled and bopped in his chair.

"Uh . . . after . . . I have a little talk with Maritza Gabriela," she said.

Uh-oh. Mami only calls me Maritza Gabriela when I'm in trouble. I had the feeling our talk wasn't going to be so "little."

DIEZ
CHAPTER 10
"SURPRISE!"

"Gabi!Gabi!Gabi!"

As Mami and I walked into the living room for our "little" talk, Miguelito ran in.

"*¡Una guagua! ¡Una guagua!*"

He was bouncing like he had springs on his feet and pointing toward the driveway. He kept screeching, "*¡Una guagua! ¡Una guagua!*" again and again.

My eardrums hurt. "A bus?" I covered my ears. "Out front?"

Miguelito nodded like crazy and tugged Mami and me by the arms to the living room window. Papi followed close behind.

In our driveway sat the airport van that picks up Mami for business trips. As we watched, the driver slid the side door open. He helped down a tall, thin lady with dark hair all rolled up in the back.

She looked kind of familiar.

I squinted. And — you won't believe this! — it was Abuelita! My grandma. Mami's mother. I hadn't seen her in a whole year.

Right behind her were Mami's brother and sister — Tío Julio and Tití Alicia!

"*¡Sorpresa!*" they yelled the moment they opened the front door. "Surprise!"

"YAAAY!" Miguelito and I shrieked.

I was so happy to see Abuelita, I practically ran down Mami and Papi getting to her.

Tío Julio flies in for business every few months. He just shows up and surprises us. Like now.

Tití Alicia lives only a few hours away so she visits a lot, too.

But we only get to see Abuelita once a year!

She scooped me up in her arms the way she used to when I was little. She's skinny, but strong. I didn't care that I'm too big to be held like Miguelito. It felt good.

"¡Oo-iii! Gabita, you've gotten so big!" Abuelita gave me a big kiss and hugged me tight.

I hugged her, too, and buried my face in her soft hair. It still smelled like I remembered. She calls it *lavanda* — lavender. It's a flower.

Tío Julio was holding Miguelito upside down and tickling his tummy. Miguelito was shrieking. "*¡No, no, Tío Julio! ¡No me haga cosquillas!* Don't tickle!"

Tío Julio made a face. "*¡Ay!* My ears! You've got a strong pair of lungs, Miguelito!"

Everyone else was hugging and kissing and laughing and talking at the same time.

Lots of loud Spanish. Lots of hands flying while talking. Abuelita finally had to put me down, so she could talk with her hands free. Nobody could hear what the other person was saying, but that didn't matter. That's the way it always is when Mami's family gets together.

While the grown-ups were all huddled up, Miguelito and I started a conga line around them. I was in the front and Miguelito was behind me, hanging on to my waist.

He and I sang: "La-la, la-la — ooo, ah!" all the way into the family room.

Then things got even louder.

"*¡Tío!¡Tío!¡Tío!*" Miguelito swung on Tío Julio's arm, trying to get his attention again. But Tío was talking to Papi about where to put all the bags.

I wanted Abuelita to know how much I liked *Brave Women in History*. I ran to my room to get it and waved it in the air.

"Abuelita! Abuelita, *¡Mira, mira!* The book you sent. I looove it!"

Mami, Abuelita, and Tití Alicia smiled and nodded at me, but everyone kept talking. I knew they heard me, though.

At last, Tío Julio and Papi took Miguelito to help carry the bags upstairs.

When things got quiet, we all sat on the couch. I snuggled between Tití Alicia and Abuelita.

Abuelita told us how Tío Julio came up with the idea to surprise us. "Julio paid me one of his famous surprise visits for my birthday. His present was this trip to California — so we could all be together."

She turned to me and stroked my face. "I'm so glad I'm here. You and Miguelito are growing up so fast! If it weren't for the pictures your *mami* sends, I'd hardly recognize you."

I hugged her.

I was glad she noticed how much I had grown in a year. Sometimes she still sends me babyish toys and clothes. But Mami and I didn't want to tell her and hurt her feelings. Maybe now she'll choose better presents. Like the book.

I looked into her eyes. It was like looking in a mirror. Abuelita has the same color eyes that I do. Gray-green with yellow speckles. It's called hazel.

But she has straight hair like Tití's, and I

68

have wavy hair. I've always wanted straight hair like theirs. Mami says mine has "body," and I'll like that when I grow up. But some mornings, my hair has so *much* body, I'm afraid it will walk off on its own!

Right then, Papi walked in carrying a tray with his *helado de coco*. He had drizzled it with *dulce de leche* — a type of caramel.

Tío Julio followed with a pot of coffee and cups.

Behind them, Miguelito balanced a bunch of spoons on a stack of napkins.

"*¡Rápido, rápido!* Quick, quick!" Miguelito said when he made it safely to the table. "*¡A comer!* Let's eat!"

Papi turned to Mami and winked. That's when I realized that Mami and Papi knew about Tío Julio's surprise visit all along. That's why Mami wanted to save the dessert for later. *That* was the surprise Miguelito heard them talking about.

The surprise for us kids!

ONCE
CHAPTER 11
A VERY ROUGH NIGHT

After dessert, we talked and talked and talked. Practically the whole night.

Miguelito fell asleep way before anyone noticed it was long past our bedtimes. So Papi took him up to his room. I made sure to be very quiet. I wanted to stay up and hear more stories about Puerto Rico, but Mami made me go to bed, too.

Even though it was very late, I couldn't sleep. I was so excited about Abuelita's visit. And I could still hear the rest of the family talking and laughing in the living room.

I could listen to them tell stories all night, if they'd let me.

Hmmm . . .

I crept out of bed and through the hallway. When no one was looking, I crawled under the dining room table and hid. Then Abuelita told a really funny story about Mami when she was little, and I laughed out loud.

That's when Mami caught me.

"Come on," she said, grinning, "off to bed. I'll tuck you in."

Once I was in bed, she sat next to me. "Gabita, always remember. No matter how angry your *papi* and I get, we'll always love you."

Then Mami gave me a big hug and kissed me good night. "Sleep well, *mi amor.*"

Still, I couldn't get to sleep. I tossed and turned and kicked the sheets off.

My brain was busy thinking: About Abuelita's surprise visit. About what Mami and Papi said. And about working with Sissy and Johnny for a whole month.

What if Johnny kept bothering me? What if all his teasing kept making me mad? Like it did on the playground with Ceci. And when I got my boots taken away.

I didn't want to think about that anymore. I was tired. I needed to get to sleep. . . .

I rolled over and turned on the radio. Maybe some music would help.

"Good night, Tipito." Tippy was snuggled on my window seat.

"Miaouu." Tippy stretched and flopped over on his side.

"Hasta mañana," I told him. "Until tomorrow. . ."

As I closed my eyes, loud Spanish voices mixed with the English words in the songs. The words got all smushed up in my brain.

The next thing I knew, a train was chugging through my bedroom.

"*RRRRR-rrrr . . . Ahhhhhh! RRRR-rrr-rrr-rr . . . Aahhhhh!*"

No . . . not a train . . . something else . . . something close by . . .

Something loud and raspy and right next to me.

Something was in bed with me!

I bolted up. I was breathing hard. My heart was pounding like bongo drums.

Then I smelled it — lavender.

"Oh, *gracias* — thank you!" I lay back down. "It's just Abuelita."

I forgot she was going to sleep with me. Tití Alicia was using the guest room. Tío Julio was in Miguelito's room. Abuelita would move to the guest room when Tití left.

She must have turned off the radio because all I could hear was "*RRRRR-rrrr . . . Ahhhhhh! . . .*"

¡Caracoles! I thought. Can you believe it? *¡Abuelita ronca!* She snores! And LOUD, too!

I tried putting my pillow over my head.

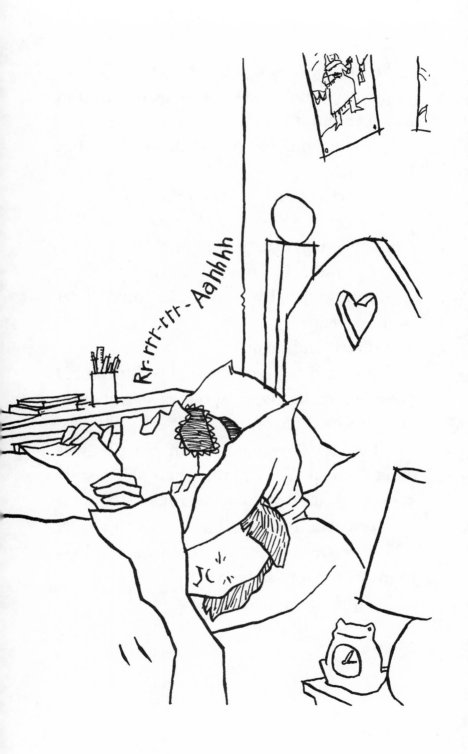

"Rr-rrr . . . Aaahh! Rr-rrr-rrr . . . Aahh!"

¡Ay, ay, ay! I could still hear her. But now I couldn't breathe.

I reached out and poked her with my toe. Just a little.

"Rr-rrr-rrr-rrr . . . Aahhhhh!"

Then she rolled over. Toward me. She took a deep breath. *"Aahhhhh!"*

After that, she stopped snoring.

But now that I was awake, I couldn't get back to sleep.

I tossed and turned.

I watched my froggie clock with the big green hands in his belly tick away the minutes. It was 2:05!

The rest of the night, when Abuelita was quiet, I slept a little. But then she'd start snoring, and I'd wake up again.

So most of the night, I lay in bed thinking.

I thought about all the mean things Johnny does and says to people.

He picked on little Ceci.

He called Devin "Metal Mouth."

And he called me Maritza Pizza and made me so mad I lost it and got my boots taken away. I even yelled at him in Spanish.

But soon, Ceci will get bigger, and he'll stop picking on her.

And next year, Devin's braces come off. Then he can't call her "Metal Mouth" anymore.

But I won't change. *I'll always be Maritza Pizza.* . . .

A car passed on the street. Its headlights lit up my wall.

I spotted my picture of Annie Oakley.

. . . *Or will I?*

I'd just thought of a perfect plan!

A perfect way to fix my worst enemy's evil ways!

DOCE
CHAPTER 12
A CRAZY MORNING

Way before I was ready the next morning, my froggie alarm began to croak: *"Rib-bit! Rib-bit! Rib-bit!"*

I rolled over and slapped the OFF button on his head.

Then my backup alarm came on: My radio blasted the D.J.'s voice in English.

And that's when the door banged open.

"¡Levántate! Get up! Get up! Get up!"

Miguelito bounced beside my bed, shaking me. He kept shrieking in Spanish. His loud shrieks hurt my ears. And the radio blared away in English.

Abuelita poked her head in and said something in Spanish about breakfast. Then she rushed back out.

"*¡Ayyyyyyyy!*" I slid out of bed and Miguelito hopped on my bare foot. "*¡Wáchate, Miguelito!*"

¿Wáchate? Is that even a word? I think I meant to say "watch out."

I put my hand on his arm and tried again. "Miguelito, *shhh. ¡Cálmate!* Calm down!"

I stumbled to my closet. I pushed aside all the piles on the floor and found my boots.

I slipped them on. They're always the first thing I put on in the morning. I think better with my boots on.

And right then, I really needed them because my head was all fuzzy-feeling and full of cotton.

I scooted Miguelito out the door, promising to play with him after school.

Then I stomped across the floor. Back and forth, back and forth. Picking out my clothes. Brushing the body out of my hair. Looking for the bathroom . . .

¡Ay, ay, ayyyyyy! The spelling test! I still had to look over my spelling words. I forgot to study them last night.

As I stumbled toward the kitchen, Tío Julio's booming voice yelled over everyone else's: "*¡Caramba!* It sounds like *un gallinero* in here!"

Un gallinero is a chicken coop. But it also means a "loony bin." Knowing Tío Julio, he probably meant the second one.

"So, Julio, does that make you *el gallo guapo*?" Tití Alicia loves to tease her brother.

Tío Julio began to strut around, flapping his elbows like a handsome rooster. Tití Alicia followed him, bobbing her head like a chicken.

Everybody laughed — even me. The kitchen sounded like three *gallineros* in one!

Then Miguelito clucked to the TV and turned up the volume. He was watching *Sesame Street*.

Now I had Spanish going in one ear and English going in the other.

"*¡Gabrielita, ven a comer!*" Abuelita had cooked breakfast and wanted me to come eat it. She put a *tortilla de guineo* on the table.

"*Tortilla de* banana, my favorite!"

I did a little hop-skip-wiggle dance in place and skipped to the table. Mami eyed my feet. She raised one eyebrow and crossed her arms. No one else noticed. They kept talking.

I looked down at my feet.

Oops! My boots. I forgot I wasn't allowed to wear them to school.

I raced back to my room and kicked them off. This time one boot did bang me on the head. *"Ow!"* I rubbed my head, and quick as a gecko, slid into my sneakers.

Just as I ran out of my room, I remembered Mr. Fine's note. I rushed back to grab it.

Back in the kitchen, I tried to enjoy my banana omelet, but my eyelids kept drooping.

Next thing I knew, Tío Julio was pulling my plate from under my face and raising my head off the table.

I couldn't believe it! I fell asleep in my *tortilla*! *¡Caracoles!* Did *I* have egg on *my* face!

I glanced at the clock. Oh, no! I was soooo late! And Papi had just left, so I couldn't get a ride with him.

I wiped my face, kissed everyone good-bye, grabbed my stuff, and raced for the door.

Halfway down the block, I remembered my lunch. I raced back home. I banged open the front door, ran for the kitchen, and tripped on the carpet. I went flying and slid across the kitchen floor on my belly.

"*¡Gabi!*" everyone screamed at the same time.

"*¿Gabi, qué pasó?*" Mami and Tío Julio rushed to my side. Tío helped me up.

"*Estoy* okay," I said. "I just tripped *en la . . . carpeta.* I forgot *mi,* uh . . . *lonche,* so I ran back . . ."

Mami checked me over and made sure I was really okay. Then she asked, "Gabi, why are you speaking Spanglish? You know that *carpeta* and *lonche* are not really Spanish words."

I blinked. I hadn't even noticed.

"I . . . uh, I tripped *en la alfombra,*" I said — the right way. *I hope.* "I forgot *mi almuerzo,* so . . ."

Abuelita grabbed my lunch bag and brought it to me. "Leave the child alone, Isa. Can't you see she's upset because she's late? Go on, Gabrielita, run along."

Abuelita walked me to the door and hugged me good-bye.

Luckily, Devin and Jasmine were still waiting at our morning meeting spot.

Jasmine took one look at me, looked down at herself, and crossed her eyes. "Did I miss an announcement?" she asked. "Is today 'Backwards Day'?"

As usual, Jasmine was perfectly dressed in a cute top with purple glitter beads and matching pants.

For the first time since I got dressed, I looked down at myself. I had on wrinkled jeans, no socks, and — you won't believe this! — the inside label on the back of my top was tickling my chin.

My shirt was on inside out and backwards!

Devin gave me a silly crooked smile —
like she wanted to laugh, but didn't want to
hurt my feelings.

"¿*Qué pasó?*" Devin glanced at Jasmine
and repeated in English. "What happened?"

I started to tell her in English — so
Jasmine could understand — but the words
kept coming out all funny. I was speaking
half English and half Spanish.

"Hey, no fair!" said Jasmine. "You guys

promised not to speak Spanish when I'm around. You know I can't understand it!"

We were late, so we started walking. Fast.

I tried telling them again. "*Mi abuelita* — my grandmother — *llegó* . . . uh . . . got here *anoche* — um, last night — and so did my *tío* and *tití*. We stayed up practically *toda la noche* talking.

"Then Abuelita *roncó, Rrrr-rrrr-rrrr* . . . *Ahhhh! Rrr-r-rrrr* . . . *Aaahh!* All night! So *me desperté*, and when I was *comiendo mi tortilla, me dormí* — I, um, fell asleep — in my eggs!"

We were almost running. I started to get a stitch in my side from walking and talking so fast.

"And the *keechena* — um, *cocina* — kitchen — was like a chicken bin — I mean, a loony coop — no, no, a loony bin! With Spanish in one ear, and *inglés* in the other . . ."

When I finished my story, I turned to Jasmine. "Jasmine?"

She wasn't there. I looked back.

She was standing on the sidewalk. Staring at us. Her mouth was hanging open.

Devin and I stopped, too. When Jasmine saw us looking, the corners of her mouth turned down. She seemed ready to cry.

Oh, no! I thought. *I've hurt her feelings.*

I shook my head. What was happening? Everything was going wrong.

I felt like those silly cartoon characters that get bonged on the head. When they wake up, they don't even know where they are.

I grabbed Devin's arm and we ran back to Jasmine.

"*Lo siento* — I mean, I'm sorry, Jasmine!" I told her. "Really! I didn't mean to make you feel left out. *No dormí* — I, uh . . . didn't get enough sleep last night. Now my tongue is all twisted!"

Jasmine blinked. She looked at me and turned to Devin. Devin shrugged.

Then — good old Jasmine! — she gave me a goofy grin. And crossed her eyes.

"Let's hurry and get to school." She pointed at the label under my chin. "You need to get to the girls' room and fix your top!"

TRECE
CHAPTER 13
MY WACKY MIXED-UP
SPANGLISH DAY!

"How about puppies?"

Later that morning in class, Sissy was reading animals off her list for our project. Our desks were pushed back into groups of three. We still didn't have a team list of animals to pick from. We spent too much time arguing yesterday.

I rolled my eyes. "Sissy, puppies are cute. But Mr. F said no farm animals or pets."

"I like pets," Sissy whined.

"I like slugs," Johnny said.

I shook my head and muttered, "You would."

Sissy and Johnny started fighting over another animal, but my head kept nodding. I was soooo sleepy. . . .

I shook my head, trying to wake up. I looked around.

In the back of the room, I spotted Melvin, the class iguana. An *un*common pet. And Mr. F did say it was okay to pick Melvin.

"Una iguana." I pointed.

"Huh?" Johnny and Sissy turned to look.

"Like Melvin," I added quickly. "We could choose *una iguana.*"

Uh-oh, I thought, *I'm doing it again.*

At least "iguana" is the same in both languages.

"No way!" Billy Wong turned to us. "*We've* got Melvin! We already voted."

Jasmine, who was in Billy's group, shrugged. Then she crossed her eyes.

I crossed my eyes back and smiled.

"Fine," I said to Billy. "Keep Melvin. We'll think of something even better."

I checked my list again. Everything was crossed off.

"I'm fresh out of animals," I told them. "How about you?"

Sissy nodded. Johnny shrugged and tossed down his pencil. I could see everything was crossed off his list, too.

"Okay," I said, "why don't we start a new list? Let's just call off animals. Sissy, you write them down. We'll choose later."

"Hey! Who made you boss?" Sissy's face got all pink and crinkled up.

I sighed. I was too pooped to start arguing again so I said, "Okaaaay . . . I'll do it."

She picked up her pencil. "No, *I'll* do it.

Because *I* want to. Not because *you* told me to."

We started calling out animals, real fast. Sissy bent over her paper, trying to keep up.

"Worms!" From Johnny.

"Kittens!" From Sissy.

"*¡Un elefante!*" *Oops!* That was me.

"Rats!" Johnny.

"Goldfish!" Sissy.

"A *jirafa!*" *Uh-oh!* Me again.

"Bats!"

"Ponies!"

"A *tortuga!*" *Yikes!* "I mean a turtle."

While we called out animals, I watched Sissy. She was busily writing down everything we said. Her perfect blond curls jiggled as she wrote. She hadn't noticed my Spanish yet.

The words were too similar to English . . . so far.

I glanced at Johnny. He was staring at me. A wide smirk spread across his face.

"Hey!" he said. "As long as we're calling out animals in Spanish, why don't we choose — what was that word? Oh, yeah . . . *moscas*. The little bugs that *fly* around Maritza Pizza!"

My face got hot enough to fry *tostones* — deep-fried green bananas.

"*¡Caracoles!*" I stomped an angry foot and glared at him.

"What's going on?" Mr. F came over.

His eyebrows flew up high above his glasses. "Maritza, do I have to write another note to your parents?"

Mr. F peered down at me over his glasses.

My heart was racing faster than a hamster on an exercise wheel.

"*Por favor*, don't do that!" My cheeks sizzled.

Finally, Mr. F sighed. "All right, Martiza. But don't make me have to warn you again," he replied. Then he did a double take. "Maritza, are you practicing your Spanish today?"

Oops! I was hoping he wouldn't notice.

Now my ears began to burn. "Umm . . . Mr. Fine, I think I'm *un poco* — uh, a little — mixed-up today. I didn't get *mucho* sleep last night."

Someone snorted. "Maritza Pizza is fried. She got left in the oven too long."

I snapped my head around. It was Johnny Wiley — who else?

"John . . ." Mr. F warned.

"That's okay, Mr. Fine." I took a deep breath. I knew I needed to use my head . . . and hold my temper.

"He doesn't bother me. *No me molesta.* Umm . . . may I tell the *clase* something?"

"Is it important?"

"*Sí, señor* — uh . . . yes, sir — *muy importante.*"

I stood and faced the class. "From now

on, *me llamo* Gabi — that's short for Gabriela, my middle *nombre* — umm . . . name. So call me Gabi.

"*Mucha gente* . . . uh . . . lots of people use their middle *nombres* — even famous *gente* like Annie Oakley. Her real *nombre* was Phoebe Anne Oakley."

I glared at Johnny. "*Ahora* . . . uh, NOW there won't be any *more* Maritza or Maritza Pizza. *¡No más!*"

I stomped a spunky foot.

That's when Johnny burst out laughing.

"Oh, even better," he said. "We've got a new kid in the class — Blabby Gabby! It's the perfect name for such a blabbermouth!"

That's when I *really* lost it. I was so sure that when I changed my name, Johnny would stop pestering me. I couldn't believe he ruined my plan.

What good is using your head if your best plans get messed up?

My boots would have worked. Spunky feet always work!

"I'm going to *agarrarte*!" I yelled at Johnny that I was going to get him.

Then I yelled all sorts of things in a mix of

Spanish and English that I don't remember. But I DO remember doing a lot of spunky-feet stomping.

And I remember that Johnny and I BOTH got one hour of detention after school . . . together!

But I guess I'd mixed in enough English that Johnny got the point. During detention he sat as far from me as possible.

I sat in the front on the left side. He sat *waaaay* in the back — on the right.

If he'd been any closer to the wall, he would have been outside.

And more *importante,* I never heard a peep out of him.

CATORCE
CHAPTER 14
VOICES OF THE COQUÍ

¡Ay, ay, ay! What a crazy mixed-up day! I thought as I walked home from school after detention.

Spanish, English! English, Spanish! Spanglish! Spanglish!

I hoped I'd never have another two days at school like the last two. EVER!

When I finally got home, nobody was there.

Strange. *Someone* should be home. Mami and Papi never leave us kids alone.

I searched the kitchen for a note.

Nada. Nothing.

I would have gotten scared, but I was too

tired. I felt like a little kid who hasn't had her nap. Good thing it was almost Saturday. I could sleep in.

I went to my room and yanked on my boots. Tired as I was, I had to figure out how to deal with Johnny Wiley and how to stop losing my temper.

Maybe a snack would help me think . . . a snack and my boots.

As I passed the family room, enjoying the feel of my boots, I heard a shout in the backyard. I ran to the sliding glass door.

And you won't believe this! Abuelita was halfway up a tall oak tree. She was sitting on a branch!

"Abuelita!" I ran outside. *"¿Qué haces?"*

Abuelita grinned. *"Un pajarito* fell out of his nest. I put him back. Just in time, too. Tippy was about to pounce on him."

She swung her legs like Miguelito does when he's happy.

Tippy watched her from the bottom of

the tree. His tail flicked back and forth like it does when he's all huffy. Then he wandered off to sulk under a bush.

"Help me down, Gabrielita," said Abuelita. Move that chair over here for me."

I dragged the chair around to the other side of the tree. Abuelita slid down the trunk like she was my age.

I held my breath until she was safely down. "Mami would be very unhappy if she knew you were climbing trees again."

Abuelita jumped off the chair. She was all surprised — like she didn't know what I was talking about. "Tree? What tree?"

At the look on my face, she winked. "Come inside, Gabrielita. I have a snack for you."

Hand in hand, we skipped into the kitchen. "Where is everybody?" I asked.

"Your *tío* had some business to take care of. And your *mami* and *tití* took Miguelito to the mall. I wanted to stay and wait for you. So we could visit." Abuelita smiled and raised one eyebrow. "Quietly."

I remembered *el gallinero* this morning and giggled.

Abuelita took a plate from the fridge.

"Yumm!" I clapped and did my hop-skip-wiggle dance. "*¡Queso blanco y pasta de guayaba!* My favorite!" I *love* white cheese and guava paste!

"I know," she said. "I brought it fresh from Puerto Rico just for you kids."

I took giant steps to the table. My boots went *kathump! kathump! kathump!* on the tile floor!

That's when Abuelita noticed my feet. "Expecting trouble?"

I giggled. "Why does everyone think there's going to be trouble if I'm wearing my boots? Sometimes I just like wearing them. They help me think."

Abuelita smiled and sat next to me.

I kept saying, "Ummm ... umm ..." I swung my spunky feet like Miguelito.

When I was done, I licked my fingers. *"Gracias, Abuelita.* That was yummy."

"Oh?" She chuckled. "I couldn't tell."

Then she put her arm around me and held me close. I breathed in her lavender smell. Today it was mixed with a little garlic from cooking.

Mami can never stop Abuelita from cooking when we're together. Mami can't stop Abuelita from doing *anything* she wants to do. Even if it's something that's not very good for her — like climbing trees.

"I've missed you, Abuelita," I said. "I'm glad you came to visit."

She kissed me on the forehead. "I've missed you, too, Gabrielita. Very much. Maybe ... maybe I'll stay a little longer this time."

"Oh, Abuelita, really? *¡Qué chévere!*" I flung my arms around her neck. "That is SO cool! We're going to have SO much fun!"

Abuelita giggled — a really silly giggle. "*Sí, Gabrielita. Lots* of fun!"

For a moment I remembered how much Abuelita snored. I wouldn't be getting much sleep after all. But she'd only be sleeping with me two more nights. Tití Alicia was going home on Sunday.

Abuelita took a flat paper bag off the table. I was too busy eating to notice it before.

"Here, Gabrielita, I brought you a present from Puerto Rico. I thought it might remind you of the times you've visited me."

Inside the bag was a music tape. But when I took it out, it wasn't music at all. It had a picture of a *coquí* on the cover and was called, *Voces del Coquí. Voices of the Coquí.*

A *coquí* is a tiny tree frog that lives only in Puerto Rico. Its job is to sing *Co-KEE! Co-KEE! Co-KEE!* each night and when it rains. That's what you hear in Puerto Rico instead of crickets.

I sighed. Everyone has a job. Even the *co-*

quí. But I wasn't doing my job right. I couldn't seem to stop using my feet and start using my head.

I turned to Abuelita. She was grinning. "Now you can fall asleep to the sound of the *coquí* singing, not your Abuelita snoring."

I felt my cheeks get warm. She knew!

I looked back at the cover. I'd never seen the word *coquí* spelled out. I put my finger on the "i" with the accent on it.

Wouldn't it be cool to have a name with an accent in it?

Then — you'll never guess! — I came up with the perfect plan to stop Johnny from teasing me about my name.

"*¡Gracias, Abuelita!*"

We gave each other a great-big, super-*abuelita*-and-*nieta* hug.

For anyone who doesn't speak-a the lingo, that's a super-grandmother-and-granddaughter hug!

QUINCE
CHAPTER 15
GET READY FOR GABÍ!

"Class," Mr. Fine began on Monday morning, "Maritza — I mean, Gabi — has two things she would like to share with us. Gabi?"

Our desks were in their usual spots — in rows facing the front. We hadn't broken up into project groups yet.

I walked to the chalkboard and in great big letters, I wrote: GaBí.

I turned to the class. "The first is that this is how you spell my name."

Jasmine grinned real big.

Devin tugged her hair.

On the board, I had put an extra big accent on the "i."

I pointed to it. "See this accent? It means that you say my name 'Ga-BEE.' Not 'GAB-bee.' And it does NOT rhyme with 'Blabby.'"

I looked at Johnny. His forehead was all crinkled, but he didn't say anything.

Devin gave her hair a double tug.

Jasmine crossed her eyes.

They both grinned.

I grinned back.

"The second thing is this tape." I held up the *coquí* tape.

First, I turned off the lights. Then I slipped the tape into Mr. F's boom box. I turned up the volume. Right away, the room was filled with tiny voices: *Co-KEE! Co-KEE! Co-KEE!*

The whole class gave a big gasp. Then they were so quiet, they seemed to be holding their breaths. It felt like we had stepped

into a rain forest . . . right in the mountains of Puerto Rico.

After a while, Sissy held up her hand.

"Sissy?" said Mr. Fine.

"What makes that pretty sound? A bird?"

Mr. Fine bowed and swished his arm at me. "Gabí?" He said it right — "Ga-BEE."

"No, that's what's so cool!" I said. "It's a tiny tree frog — half the size of my pinkie!"

I turned the lights back on and held up my little finger.

Everyone gasped again.

"You want to see a picture?" I held up the cover of the tape.

Everyone leaned forward in their desks.

"I can't see! I can't see!" they said.

Johnny raised his hand. "Mr. Fine, can I pass it around so everyone can see it?"

"*May* I," said Mr. F. Then he turned to me. "Gabí? Is that all right?"

"Oh . . . um . . ."

Johnny leaned way into his desk. He reminded me of a puppy waiting for a treat.

"Oh, okay," I said.

Johnny bounced to my side. He looked down at the picture of the tiny brown frog sitting inside a big red flower.

He sucked in his breath.

"Cool," he whispered. "Very cool."

I'd never stood so close to Johnny before.

And I'd never heard him whisper.

It made me listen — the way Mami had made me listen when I was little, just by whispering. And what I heard was someone who wasn't *all* nasty.

"Do you think we could do our animal project on the *coquí*?" he asked me.

My mouth fell open. "Uh . . . sure. But we have to ask Sissy."

Johnny took the picture to Sissy. "What do you think?"

Sissy stared at it for a long time. Then she whispered, too. I think she said, "Cool."

"Are you with us?" Johnny asked her. "Want to do our project on the *coquí*?"

"Yeah," she said. "That would be *way* cool." And she smiled at me.

Johnny took back the picture and stared at it again. "Hey! Look at this! The *coquí* spells its name the same way Gabí does. With an accent on the "i."

And you won't believe what he said next!

"You even say it the same way. Ga-BEE. Co-KEE." He grinned. "Gabí the *coquí*!"

I slapped my forehead.

I looked at Devin. She was biting her lips together, trying not to laugh.

I looked at Jasmine. She squeezed her eyes shut and put her hand over her mouth.

I looked at Mr. Fine. His upper lip was twitching.

Suddenly, I started laughing. I laughed and I laughed and I laughed.

And the whole class laughed with me.

Everyone but Johnny. His mouth was hanging open.

Now I grinned. Real big. "If Gabí the *coquí* is all you can call me, that's okay. In fact, it's better than okay. I LIKE it!"

*   *   *

As I raced home after school, I sang to myself: *I did it! I did it! I DID IT!*

I spoiled my worst enemy's evil plans. And I did it with my head — not my spunky feet. So I never gave away my secret identity. Or got in trouble.

I ran inside and pulled on my boots.

My RED boots.

With the white moons and stars carved on the sides.

I stomped around my room.

I jumped on the bed. Boots and all.

"Watch out, world!" I yelled. "Bullies be warned! Get ready for Gabí!

"*¡Gabí está aquí!*"

¡HABLA ESPAÑOL!
(That means: *Speak Spanish!*)

abuelita (ah-booeh-LEE-tah): grandma

ají (ah-HEE): chili pepper

ajo (AH-hoh): garlic

alfombra (ahl-FOHM-brah): carpet, rug

almuerzo (ahl-MOOWEHR-soh): lunch

amor (ah-MOHR): love

bobo (BOH-boh): silly, foolish

botas (BOH-tahs): boots

cálmate (KAHL-mah-teh): calm down

¡Caracoles! (kah-rah-KOH-lehs): snails; can also be used to mean "Yikes!" or "Wow!" or "Doggone it!"

chévere (CHEH-behr-eh): Cool!

cocina (koh-SEE-nah): kitchen

coco (KOH-koh): coconut

comer (koh-MEHR): to eat

congelador (kohn-heh-lah-DOHR): freezer

contento (kohn-TEN-toh): happy

cuchichear (koo-chee-cheh-AHR): to whisper

dormir (dohr-MEER): to sleep

elefante (eh-leh-FAHN-teh): elephant

gente (HEN-teh): people

gracias (GRAH-seeyahs): thank you

guagua (GOOWAH-goowah): bus or van

hamburguesa (ahm-buhr-GEH-sah): hamburger

helado (eh-LAH-doh): ice cream

hija (EE-hah): daughter

importante (eem-pohr-TAN-teh): important

inglés (een-GLEHS): English

jirafa (hee-RAH-fah): giraffe

leche (LEH-cheh): milk

lo siento (loh SEEYEN-toh): I am sorry.

mala / malo (MAH-lah / MAH-loh): bad

¡mira! (MEE-rah): Look!

mosca (MOHS-kah): fly

muchacha (moo-CHAH-chah): girl

muchacho (moo-CHAH-cho): boy

muy bueno (moowee BOOEH-noh): very good

nada (NAH-dah): nothing

nieta (NEEYEH-tah): granddaughter

noche (NOH-cheh): night

nombre(s) (NOHM-breh(s)): name(s)

oreja (oh-REH-hah): ear

pajarito (pah-hah-REE-toh): little bird; baby bird

papas fritas (PAH-pahs FREE-tahs): french fries

perro (PEH-rroh): dog

picante (pee-KAN-teh): spicy hot

platos (PLAH-tohs): plates

por favor (pohr fah-VOHR): please

¿Qué? (KEH): What?

¿Qué haces? (KEH AH-sehs): What are you doing?

¿Qué pasa? (KEH PAH-sah): What's going on?; What's happening?; What's up?

Te quiero (teh KEEYEH-roh): I love you.

rabo (RAH-boh): tail

rana (RAH-nah): frog

rápido (RAH-pee-doh): quickly

roncar (rohn-KAHR): to snore

no sé (noh SEH): I don't know.

sí (SEE): yes

sorpresa (sohr-PREH-sah): surprise

tía (TEE-ah): aunt; **tío** (TEE-oh): uncle

tití (tee-TEE): auntie

tortilla de guineo (tohr-TEE-yah deh gee-NEH-oh): banana omelet

tortuga (tohr-TOO-gah): turtle; tortoise

#2 Who's That Girl?

I smiled as I peddled my bike down the sidewalk to the new neighbor's house.

Miguelito peddled beside me on his big blue plastic tricycle. It made a huge racket that I was trying to ignore.

Soon we reached the end of the block.

"*¡Mira! ¡Mira!*" Miguelito pointed to the big truck. "*¡El camión!*"

"*Shhh!* I see it. Remember what we said about being *quiet*?"

Miguelito put his pudgy finger on his lips. "Shhh, very *quiet*," he whispered.

The back doors of the truck were open. A big, old ramp ran down the back of the truck to the street.

Two huge men were carrying a couch down the ramp.

I glanced around. The front double doors of the house were open. But the house was dark inside. I couldn't see the new neighbors.

I looked for signs of kids. Lots of big boxes were stacked on the lawn. But no toys or bicycles . . .

"Careful, kids," one of the big men said. "Stay clear of the truck . . ."

"Are you the new neighbor?" I asked.

"Nah, kid. I'm just one of the movers. The new owners aren't here yet. Real estate lady let us in."

"Oh," I said. "When will they move in?"

"Not my business." He put down the box to wipe his face. He was all sweaty.

"Do they have kids?" Miguelito asked.

"You kids are full of questions, aren't you?"

Miguelito nodded. "There's lots we want to know."

The man laughed. "Yeah, kid. Me, too. Like sometimes I want to know what's the point?"

"Huh?" Miguelito and I said. Some grown-ups are really weird.

"Yeah, honey. *Huh?* That's what I say."

The man picked up the box and took it inside.

We waited another minute. When no one else came out of the house, I glanced around. No one was looking.

"Stay right here, Miguelito. Don't move."

I stepped to the back of the truck. I peeked inside.

Way in the back were three bicycles: two big boys' bikes and one small one.

And you won't believe this! The small one was just like mine.

But it was pink and purple.

A girl's bike!

To our lovely Adi,

    We hope you enjoy the last Faraway Tree book + remember it forever.

        love

    Lauren, Ra'anan, Rachel

    Sarah + Nathan.

P.S. Thanks for coming to visit us in Australia. We loved having you here Please come visit again soon.

The Folk of the Faraway Tree

By Enid Blyton

HINKLER
BOOKS

The Folk of the Faraway Tree
By Enid Blyton

First published in Great Britain 1946 by Newnes
This edition published 2003 by
Hinkler Books Pty Ltd
17–23 Redwood Drive
Dingley VIC 3172
Australia
www.hinklerbooks.com
Published by arrangement with Egmont Books Ltd, London.

www.blyton.com

10 9 8 7 6 5 4
10 09 08 07

ISBN 1 8651 5955 7

Printed & bound Australia

The Author
Enid Blyton

Enid Blyton is one of the best-loved writers of the twentieth century. Her wonderful, inventive stories, plays and poems have delighted children of all ages for generations.

Born in London in 1897, Enid Blyton sold her first piece of literature; a poem entitled 'Have You ...?', at the age of twenty. She qualified and worked as a teacher, writing extensively in her spare time. She sold short stories and poems to various magazines and her first book, *Child Whispers*, was published in 1922.

Over the next 40 years, Blyton would publish on average fifteen books a year. Some of her more famous works include Noddy, The Famous Five, The Secret Seven and The Faraway Tree series.

Her books have sold in the millions and have been translated into many languages. Enid Blyton married twice and had two daughters. She died in 1968, but her work continues to live on.

Contents

Up and away.

Curious Connie Comes to Stay

One day Mother came to the three children, as they worked out in the garden, and spoke to them.

'Joe! Beth! Frannie! Listen to me for a minute. I've just had a letter from an old friend of mine, and I'm wondering what to do. I'll read it to you.'

Mother read the letter:

'DEAR OLD FRIEND,

'Please will you do something for me? I have not been well for some time, and the doctor says I must go away on a long holiday. But, as you know, I have a little girl, Connie, and I cannot leave her by herself. So would you please let her stay with you until I come back? I will, of course, pay you well.

'Your three children are good and well behaved, and I feel that their friendship will be very good for my little Connie, who is, I am afraid, rather spoilt. Do let me know soon.

'Your old friend,
'LIZZIE HAYNES.'

The three children listened in silence. Then Beth spoke.

'Oh, Mother! We've seen Connie once, and she was very selfish and spoilt—and so curious too, sticking her nose into everything! Have we got to have her?'

'No, of course not,' said Mother. 'But I could do with some extra money, you know—and I do think Connie would soon settle down and stop being spoilt if she lived with us. It would be good for her!'

'And I suppose we should help people if we can,' said Joe. 'All right, Mother—we'll have Connie, shall we, and just teach her not to be spoilt!'

'We'll be able to show her the Enchanted Wood and the Faraway Tree!' said Frannie.

'Yes—we used to have our cousin Rick, but now he's gone back home,' said Beth. 'We'll have Connie instead! If you put a little bed into the corner of Frannie's and my room, Mother, we can have her in there.'

Mother smiled at them and went indoors to write to her old friend, to say yes, she would have Connie. The children looked at one another.

'We'll soon tick Connie off if she starts any of her high-and-mighty ways here,' said Beth.

'And we'll stop her poking her nose into everything too!' said Frannie. 'Well—what about taking her up the Faraway Tree and letting her peep in at the Angry Pixie? He'll soon tick her off!'

The others giggled. They could see that they would have a bit of fun with Connie. She was always so curious and inquisitive about everything and everyone. Well—she would get a few shocks in the Enchanted Wood!

'It will be fun showing somebody else the Faraway Tree, and all the people there,' said Joe. 'I wonder what Curious Connie will think of the Saucepan Man, and Silky and Moon-Face!'

'And I wonder what they will think of her!' said Beth. 'What a lovely name for her, Joe—Curious Connie! I'll always think of her like that now!'

Curious Connie was to come the next week. Beth helped Mother put a little bed into the corner of the girls' bedroom. Connie wasn't very big. She was the same age as Frannie, but she was a fussy eater, and hadn't grown as big as Frannie. She was a pretty, dainty little thing, who liked wearing nice clothes.

'Brush that untidy hair, Frannie, before you meet Connie,' said Mother. Frannie's hair had grown rather long, and needed a trim.

The children went to meet the bus. 'There it is!' cried Joe. 'Coming round the corner. And there's Curious Connie on it, look—all dressed up as if she was going to a party!'

Connie jumped off the bus, carrying a bag. Joe politely took it from her, and gave her a welcoming kiss. The girls welcomed her too. Connie looked them up and down.

'Huh, you do look like country kids!' she said.

'Well, that's what we are,' said Beth. 'You'll look like us soon, too. I hope you'll be very happy here, Connie.'

'I saw Rick the other day,' said Connie, as she walked daintily along the lane with the others. 'He told me the most ridiculous stories!'

3

'Rick did! But he's not a story-teller!' said Joe, in surprise. 'What sort of stories did he tell you?'

'Well, he told me about a silly Enchanted Wood and a ridiculous Faraway Tree, and some stupid people called Moon-Face and Dame Washalot and Mister Watzisname, and a crazy fellow called the Saucepan Man who was deaf,' said Connie.

'Oh! Do you think all those were silly and stupid?' said Joe at last.

'I didn't believe in any of it,' said Connie. 'I don't believe in things like that—fairies or elves or magic or anything. It's old fashioned.'

'Well, we must be very old fashioned then,' said Beth. 'Because we not only believe in the Enchanted Wood and the Faraway Tree and love our funny friends there, but we go to see them too—and we visit the lands at the top of the Tree as well! We did think of taking you too!'

'It wouldn't be much use,' said Connie. 'I won't believe in them at all.'

'What—not even if you saw them?' cried Frannie.

'I don't think so,' said Connie. 'I mean—it all sounds quite impossible to me. Really it does.'

'Well, we'll see,' said Joe. 'It looks as if we'll have some fun with you, up the Faraway Tree, Connie! I would like to see the Angry Pixie's face if you tell him you don't believe in him!'

'Let's take her tomorrow!' said Beth, with a giggle.

'All right!' said Joe. 'But we'd better not let her go into any land at the top of the Tree. She'd never get down again!'

'What land? At the top of the tree? A land at the top of a tree!' said Connie, puzzled.

'Yes,' said Beth. 'You see, the Enchanted Wood is quite near here, Connie. And in the middle of it is the biggest, tallest tree in the world—very magic. It's called the Faraway Tree, because its top is so far away, and always sticks up into some strange magic land there—a different one every week.'

'I don't believe a word of it,' said Connie.

'All right. Don't, then,' said Frannie, beginning to feel angry. 'Look—here we are, home—and there's

'I don't believe in things like that.'

5

Mother looking out for us!'

Soon Connie and the girls were unpacking Connie's bag and putting her things away into two empty drawers in the bedside cabinet. Beth saw that there were no really sensible country clothes at all. However could Connie climb the Faraway Tree in a flimsy dress? She should have some old clothes! Well, she and Frannie had plenty so they could lend her some.

'I suppose you are longing to show Connie the Enchanted Wood!' said Mother, when they went down to dinner.

'Oh—do you believe in it too?' said Connie, surprised that a grown-up should do so.

'Well, I haven't seen the Tree, but I have seen some of the people that come down it,' said Mother.

'Look—here's one of them now!' said Joe, jumping up as he saw someone coming in at the front gate. It was Moon-Face, his round face beaming happily. He carried a note in his hand.

'Hello!' said Joe, opening the door. 'Come in and have some dinner, Moon-Face. We've got a little friend here—the girl I was telling you about—Connie.'

'Ah—how do you do?' said Moon-Face, going all polite as he saw the dainty, pretty Connie. 'I've come to ask you to dinner with me and Silky tomorrow, Connie. I hope you can come. Any friend of the children's is welcome up the Faraway Tree!'

Connie shook hands with the strange, round-faced little man. She hardly knew what to say. If she said she would go to dinner with him she was as good as saying that she believed in all this nonsense about the Faraway

6

Tree — and she certainly didn't!

'Moon-Face, you have put poor Connie into a fix,' said Joe, grinning. 'She doesn't believe in you, you see — so how can she come to dinner with a person she doesn't believe in, at a place she thinks isn't there?'

'Quite easily,' said Moon-Face. 'Let her think it is a dream. Let her think I'm a dream.'

'All right,' said Connie, who really was longing to go to dinner with him, after all she had said. 'All right. I'll come. I'll think you're just a dream. You probably are, anyway.'

'And I'll think you are a dream too,' said Moon-Face politely. 'Then it will be nice for both of us.'

'Well, I'm not a dream!' said Connie, rather indignantly. 'I should have thought you could see quite well I'm real, and not a dream.'

Moon-Face grinned. 'I hope you're a good dream, and not a bad one, if you are a dream,' he said. 'Well — see you all tomorrow. Four o'clock, in my house at the top of the Tree. Will you walk up, or shall I send down cushions on a rope for you?'

'We'll walk up,' said Joe. 'We really want Connie to meet the people who live in the tree. She won't believe in any of them, but they'll believe in her all right — and it might be rather funny!'

'It certainly will!' said Moon-Face, and went off, grinning again, leaving Silky's polite invitation note in Connie's small hand.

'I'm not sure I like him very much,' said Connie, taking the last bun off the plate.

'What — not like Moon-Face!' cried Frannie, who

really loved the strange little man. 'He's the dearest, kindest, funniest, nicest—'

'All right, all right,' said Connie. 'Don't go on for hours like that. I'll go tomorrow—but I still say it's all make-believe and pretence, and not really real!'

'You wait and see!' said Joe. 'Come on—we've time for a game before bed ... and tomorrow, Connie, tomorrow, you will go up the Faraway Tree!'

Up the Faraway Tree

The next day was bright and sunny. Connie woke up feeling rather excited. She was away from home, staying in the country—she had three playmates—and they had promised to take her up the Faraway Tree!

'Even if I don't believe in it, it will be fun to see what they think it is,' she said to herself. 'I hope we have a good time, and a nice dinner.'

The children usually had to do some kind of work in the mornings, even though it was holiday time. Beth and Frannie decided to help their mother, while Joe helped Father in the garden. There was a good deal to do there, because there had been some rain, and the weeds had come up by the hundred.

Connie didn't like having to help make the beds very much, but the children's mother was quite firm with her.

'You will do the same as the others,' she said. 'And don't pout like that, Connie. I don't like it. It makes you look ugly.'

Connie was not used to being spoken to like this. Her mother had always fussed round her and spoilt her, and she had been the one and only child in the house. Now she was one of four, and things were very different.

'Cheer up!' said Beth, seeing tears in Connie's eyes.

'Don't be a spoilt baby! Think of our treat this afternoon!'

Connie sniffed. 'Funny sort of treat!' she said, but all the same she did cheer up.

When three o'clock came Mother said the children could go. 'It will take you some time to get up the Tree, I am sure, if you are going to show Connie everything,' she said. 'And please don't let her get wet with Dame Washalot's water, will you?'

Connie looked up in surprise. 'Dame Washalot's water!' she said. 'Whatever do you mean?'

Beth giggled. 'There's an old woman who lives up the Tree, who is always washing,' she said. 'She just adores washing, and when she has finished she tips up her wash-tub, and the soapy water comes sloshing down the tree. You have to look out for it.'

'I don't believe a word of it!' said Connie, and she didn't. 'Doing washing up a tree! It sounds quite daft to me.'

'Let's go now,' said Beth, 'or we won't be at Moon-Face's by four o'clock.'

'I must go and change into a pretty dress,' said Connie.

'No, don't,' said Frannie. 'Go as you are. We don't change into nice clothes when we go up the Tree.'

'What—go out to dinner in ordinary clothes!' cried Connie. 'I just couldn't!' And off she went to put on a clean, white dress.

They all went to the edge of the Wood. There was a ditch there. 'Jump over this—and you're in the Enchanted Wood!' said Beth.

They all jumped, Connie too. As soon as she was across the ditch, and heard the trees whispering, 'wisha, wisha, wisha,' as they always did in the Enchanted Wood, Connie felt different. She felt excited and curious and happy. She felt as if there was magic about—although she didn't believe in magic! It was a really lovely feeling.

They went through the wood, and came to an enormous tree, with a tremendously thick and knotted trunk. Connie gazed up into the branches.

'Gosh!' she said. 'I've never seen such a tree before! Is this the Magic Faraway Tree? How marvellous!'

'Yes,' said Joe, enjoying Connie's surprise. 'And at the top, as we told you, there is a different land every week. I don't know what land is there now. We don't always go. Sometimes the lands aren't very nice. Once there was the Land of Bad Temper. That was horrid. And a little while ago there was the Land of Punishments. We didn't go there, you can guess! We asked our friends Silky and Moon-Face what it was like, and they said they didn't know either, but they could hear shouts and cries going on all the time!'

'Gosh!' said Connie, alarmed. 'I wouldn't like to go to a land like that. Although, of course,' she added quickly, 'I don't believe in such a thing.'

'Of course you don't,' said Joe, with a grin. 'You don't believe in the Faraway Tree either, do you? And yet you are going to climb it. Come on—up we go!'

They swung themselves up on the lower branches. It was a very easy tree to climb. The branches were broad and strong, and so many little folk walked up and down the Tree all day long that little paths had been worn on the broad boughs.

'What sort of tree is it?' said Connie. 'It looks like a cherry tree to me. Oh, look—there are some ripe cherries—just out of my reach, though. Never mind, I'll pick some further up.'

'Better pick them now, or you may find the Tree is growing walnuts a bit higher up,' said Beth, laughing. 'It's a magic Tree, you know. It grows all kinds of different things at any time!'

Sure enough, when Connie looked for ripe cherries a little way up, she found, to her surprise, that the Tree was now growing horse-chestnut leaves and had prickly covered horse chestnuts! She was surprised and disappointed—and very puzzled. Could it really be a magic tree, then?

Soon they met all kinds of little folk coming down the Tree. There were elves and pixies, a goblin or two, a few rabbits and one or two squirrels. It was odd to see a rabbit up a tree. Connie blinked her eyes to see if she really was looking at rabbits up a tree, but there was no doubt about it; she was. The funny thing was, they were dressed in clothes too. That was odder than ever.

'Do people live in this tree?' asked Connie, in wonder, as they came to a little window in the big trunk.

'Oh yes—lots of them,' said Joe. 'But don't go peeping into that window, now, Connie. The Angry Pixie lives inside the little house there, and he does hate people to peep in.'

'All right, I won't peep,' said Connie, who was very curious indeed to know what the little house looked

12

like. She meant to peep, of course. She was far too inquisitive a little girl not to do a bit of prying, if she had the chance!

'My shoe-lace is undone,' she called to the others. 'You go on ahead, I'll follow.'

'I bet she wants to peep,' whispered Joe to Beth, with a grin. 'Come on! Let her!'

They went on to a higher branch. Connie pretended to fiddle about with her shoe, and then, when she saw that the others were a little way up, she climbed quickly over to the little window.

She peeped inside. Oh, what fun! Oh, how lovely! There was a proper little room inside the tree, with a bed and a chair and a table. Sitting writing at the table was the Angry Pixie, his glasses on his nose. He had an enormous ink pot full of ink, and a very small pen, and his fingers were stained with the purple ink.

Connie's shadow at the window made him look up. He saw the little girl there, peeping, and he flew into one of his tempers. He shot to his feet, picked up the enormous ink pot and rushed to his window. He opened it and yelled loudly:

'Peeping again! Everybody peeps in at my window, everybody! I won't have it! I really won't have it.'

He emptied the ink pot all over the alarmed Connie. The ink fell in big spots on her clothes, and on her cheeks and hands. She was in a terrible mess.

'Oh! Oh! You wicked thing!' she cried. 'Look what you've done to me.'

'Well, you shouldn't peep,' cried the Angry Pixie, still in a rage. 'Now I can't finish my letter. I've got no

13

more ink! You bad girl! You horrid peeper!'

'Joe! Beth! Come and help me!' sobbed Connie, crying tears of anger and despair down her ink-smudged cheeks.

The Angry Pixie suddenly looked surprised and a little ashamed. 'Oh—are you a friend of Joe's?' he asked. 'Why didn't you say so? I would have shouted at you for peeping, but I wouldn't have thrown ink at you. Really, I wouldn't. Joe should have warned you not to peep.'

'I did,' said Joe, appearing at the window, too. 'It's her own fault. My, you do look a mess, Connie. Come on! We'll never be at Moon-Face's by four o'clock.'

Wiping away her tears, Connie followed the others up the Tree. They came to another window, and this time the three children looked in—but Connie wouldn't. 'No thank you,' she said. 'I'm not going to have things thrown at me again. I think the people who live here are horrid.'

'You needn't be afraid of peeping in at this window,' said Joe. 'The Owl lives here and he always sleeps in the day time, so he never sees people peeping in. He's a great friend of Silky the fairy. Look at him lying asleep on his bed. That red night-cap he's got on was knitted for him by Silky. Doesn't he look nice in it?'

But Connie wouldn't look in. She was angry and sulky. She went on up the Tree by herself. Joe suddenly heard a sound he knew very well, and he yelled loudly to Connie:

'Hey, Connie, Connie, look out! I can hear Dame Washalot's water coming down the tree. LOOK OUT!'

Connie was just about to answer that she didn't believe in Dame Washalot, or her silly water, when a cascade of dirty, soapy water came splashing down the Faraway Tree! It fell all over poor Connie, and soaked her from head to foot! Some of the suds stayed in her hair, and she looked a dreadful sight.

The others had all ducked under broad boughs as soon as they heard the water coming, and they didn't get a drop on them. Joe began to laugh when he saw Connie. The little girl burst into tears again.

'Let me go home, let me go home!' she wept. 'I hate your Faraway Tree. I hate all the people in it! Let me go home!'

A silvery voice called down the Tree. 'Who's in trouble? Come up and I'll help you!'

'It's dear Silky!' said Beth. 'Come on, Connie. She'll get you dry again!'

Connie Meets a Few People

'I don't want to see any more of the horrid people who live in this tree,' wept poor Connie. But Joe took her firmly by the hand and pulled her up a broad bough to where a yellow door stood open in the Tree.

In the doorway stood the prettiest little fairy you ever saw. She had hair that stood out round her head like a golden mist, as fine as silk. She held out her hand to Connie.

'Poor child! Did you get caught in Dame Washalot's water! She has been washing such a lot today, and the water has been coming down all day long! Let me dry you.'

Connie couldn't help liking this pretty little fairy. How dainty she was in her shining dress, and what tiny feet and hands she had!

Silky drew her into her tidy little house. She took a towel from a peg and began to dry Connie. The others told her who she was.

'Yes, I know,' said Silky. 'We're going up to Moon-Face's house for dinner. He said he would ask Mister Watzisname too, but I don't expect he'll come, because I heard him snoring in his chair as usual a little while ago.'

Connie Meets a Few People

'Mister who?' asked Connie.

'Mister Watzisname,' said Silky. 'He doesn't know his name nor does anyone else, so we call him Watzisname. We've tried and tried to find out what his name is, but I don't expect we shall ever know now. Unless the Land of Know-All comes—then we might go up there and find out. You can find out anything in the Land of Know-All.'

'Oh!' said Joe, thinking of a whole lot of things he would love to know. 'We'll go there if it comes.'

Suddenly, there came a curious noise down the Tree—a clanking and jingling, crashing and banging. Connie looked scared. Whatever would happen next? It sounded as if a hundred saucepans, a few dozen kettles, and some odds and ends of dishes and pans were all falling down the Tree together!

Then a voice came floating down the Tree, and the children grinned.

> 'Two books for a book-worm,
> Two butts for a goat,
> Two winks for a winkle
> Who can't sing a note!'

'What a very silly song!' said Connie.

'Yes, isn't it?' said Joe. 'It's the kind the Old Saucepan Man always sings. It's his 'Two' song. Every line but the last begins with the word 'Two'. Anyone can make up a song like that.'

'Well, I'm sure I don't want to,' said Connie, thinking that everyone in the Faraway Tree must be a bit crazy.

'Who's the Saucepan Man? And what's that awful crashing noise?'

'Only his saucepans and kettles and things,' said Beth. 'He carries them round with him. He's a dear. Once we saw him without his saucepans and things round him, and we didn't know him. He looked funny—quite different.'

A very extraordinary person now came into Silky's tiny house, almost getting stuck in the door. He was covered from head to toe with saucepans, kettles and pans, which were tied round him with string. They jangled and crashed together, so everyone always knew when the Saucepan Man was coming.

Connie stared at him, amazed. His hat was a very big saucepan, so big that it hid most of his face. Connie could see a wide grin, but that was about all.

'Who's this funny creature?' said Connie, in a loud and rather rude voice.

Now the Saucepan Man was deaf, and he didn't usually hear what was said—but this time he did, and he didn't like it. He tilted back his saucepan hat and stared at Connie.

'Who's this dirty little girl?' he said, in a voice just as loud as Connie's. Connie went red. She glared at the Saucepan Man.

'This is Connie,' said Joe. He turned to Connie. 'This is Saucepan, a great friend of ours,' he said. 'We've had lots of adventures together.'

'Why is she so dirty?' asked Saucepan, looking at Connie's ink-stained clothes and dirty face. 'Is she always like that? Why don't you clean her up?'

Connie was furious. She was always so clean and

dainty and well dressed—how dare this horrid clanking little man talk about her like that!

'Go away!' she said, angrily.

'Yes, it's a very nice day,' said the Saucepan Man, politely, going suddenly deaf.

'Don't stay here and STARE!' shouted Connie.

'I certainly should wash your hair,' said the Saucepan Man at once. 'It's full of soap suds.'

'I said, "Don't STARE!"' cried Connie.

'Mind that stair?' said the Saucepan Man, looking round. 'Can't see any. Didn't know there were any stairs in the Faraway Tree.'

Connie stared at him in rage. 'Is he crazy?' she said to Joe.

Joe and the others were laughing at this peculiar conversation. Joe shook his head. 'No, Saucepan isn't crazy. He's just deaf. His saucepans make such a clanking all the time that the noise gets into his ears, and he can't hear properly. So he keeps making mistakes.'

'That's right,' said the Saucepan Man, entering into the conversation suddenly. 'Cakes. Plenty of them. Waiting for us at Moon-Face's.'

'I said "Mistakes",' said Joe. 'Not cakes.'

'But Moon-Face's cakes aren't mistakes,' said Saucepan, earnestly.

Joe gave it up. 'We'd better go up to Moon-Face's,' he said. 'It's past four o'clock.'

'I hope that awful Saucepan Man isn't coming with us,' said Connie. Incredibly, Saucepan heard what she said. He looked angry.

'I hope this nasty little girl isn't coming with us,' he

said, in his turn, and glared at Connie.

'Now, now, now,' said Silky, and patted the Saucepan Man on one of his kettles. 'Don't get angry. It only makes things worse.'

'Purse? Have you lost it?' said the Saucepan Man, anxiously.

'I said "worse" not "purse",' said Silky. 'Come on! Let's go. Connie's dry now, but I can't get the ink stains out of her dress.'

They all began to climb the Tree again, the Saucepan Man making an appalling noise. He began to sing his silly song.

'Two bangs for a firework,
Two . . .'

'Be quiet!' said Silky. 'You'll wake Mister Watzisname. He's fast asleep. He went to bed very late last night, so he'll be tired. We won't wake him. We'll be dreadfully squashed inside Moon-Face's house anyhow. Creep past his chair quietly. Saucepan, try not to make your kettles clang together.'

'Yes, lovely weather,' agreed Saucepan, mishearing again. They all crept past. Saucepan made a few clatters, but they didn't disturb Watzisname, who snored loudly and peacefully in his chair on the broad bough of the Tree outside his house. His mouth was wide open.

'You'd expect people would pop things in his mouth if he leaves it open like that,' whispered Connie.

'People do,' said Joe. 'Moon-Face put some acorns in once. Watzisname was very angry. He really was. It's a wonder he doesn't get soaked with Dame Washalot's water, but he doesn't seem to. He always puts his chair well under that big branch.'

They went on up the Tree. In the distance they saw Dame Washalot, hanging out some clothes on boughs. 'They blow away if she doesn't get someone to sit on them,' said Silky to Connie. 'So she pays the baby squirrels to sit patiently on each bit of washing she does till it's dry and she can take it in and iron it.'

'They saw the line of baby squirrels in the distance. They looked sweet. Connie wanted to go nearer, but Joe said no, they really must go on; Moon-Face would be tired of waiting for them.

At last they came almost to the top of the Tree. Connie was amazed when she looked down. The Faraway Tree rose higher than any other tree in the Enchanted Wood. Far below them waved the tops of other trees. The Faraway Tree was really wonderful.

'Here we are, at Moon-Face's,' said Joe, and he banged on the door. It flew open and Moon-Face looked out, his big round face one large smile.

'I thought you were never coming!' he said. 'You are late!'

'We've brought this dirty little girl,' said Saucepan, and he pushed Connie forward.

Moon-Face looked at her.

'She does look a bit dirty,' he said, and smiled broadly. 'I suppose she got into trouble with the Angry Pixie—and got some of Dame Washalot's water on her too! Never mind! Come along in and we'll have a good meal. I've got some Hot-Cold Goodies!'

'Whatever are they?' said Connie, and even the others hadn't heard of them.

They all went into Moon-Face's exciting house. It was quite extraordinary. In the very middle was a large hole, with a pile of coloured cushions by it. Round the hole was Moon-Face's furniture, all curved to fit the roundness of the tree trunk. There was a curious curved bed, a curved sofa, and a curved stove and chairs, all set round the trunk inside the Tree.

'It's very exciting,' said Connie, looking round. 'What's that hole in the middle?'

Nobody answered her. They were too busy looking at the lovely food that Moon-Face had put ready on the curved table. They wanted to know what the Hot-Cold Goodies were like. They knew Pop Cakes and Google Buns—but they didn't know Hot-Cold Goodies.

'What's this hole?' demanded Connie again, but no one bothered about her. She felt so curious that she went to the edge of the strange hole, and put her foot in it to see if there were steps down. She suddenly lost her balance, and stepped right into the hole! She sat down with a bump—and then, oh my goodness! She began to slide away at top speed down the hole that ran from the top of the Tree to the bottom!

'Where's Connie?' said Joe, suddenly, looking round.

'Not here. That's good!' said Saucepan.

'She must have fallen down the slippery-slip!' said Silky. 'Oh, poor Connie—she'll be at the bottom of the Tree by now! We'll have to go down and get her!'

Dinner with Moon-Face

Connie was frightened when she found herself slipping down the hole in the Tree. Usually people who used the slippery-slip had a cushion to sit on, but Connie hadn't. She slid down and down and round and round, faster and faster. She gasped, and her hair flew out behind her.

She came to the bottom of the Tree, and her feet touched a little trap door set in the side there. It flew open and Connie shot out, landing on a soft tuft of moss, which the little folk grew there specially, so that anyone using the tree slide would land softly.

Connie landed on the moss and sat there, gasping and scared. She was at the bottom of the tree! The others were all at the top! They would be having dinner together, laughing and joking. They wouldn't miss her. She would have to stay at the bottom of the tree till they came down again, and that might not be for ages.

'If I knew the way home I'd go,' thought Connie. 'But I don't. Oh—what's that?'

It was a red squirrel, dressed in an old sweater. He came out of a hole in the trunk, where he lived. He bounded over to Connie.

'Where's your cushion, please?' he said.

'What cushion?' said Connie.

'The one you slid down on,' said the squirrel.

'I didn't slide down on one,' said Connie.

'You must have,' said the red squirrel, looking all round for a cushion. 'People always do. Where have you put it? Don't be a naughty girl now. Let me have it. I always have to take them back to Moon-Face.'

'I tell you I didn't have a cushion,' said Connie, beginning to feel annoyed. 'I just slid down without one, and I got pretty warm.'

She stood up. The squirrel looked at the back of her. 'My! You've worn out the back of your dress, sliding down without a cushion,' he said. 'It's all in rags. Your underwear is showing.'

'Oh! This is a horrible afternoon!' said poor Connie. 'I've been splashed with ink and soaked with soapy water, and now I've worn out the back of my dress.'

The trap door suddenly shot open again and out flew Moon-Face on one of his cushions. He shouted to Connie.

'Well! Didn't you like my party? Why did you rush off so quickly?'

'I fell down that silly hole,' said Connie. 'Look at the back of my dress.'

'There's nothing to look at. You've worn it out, slipping down without a cushion,' said Moon-Face. 'Come on, I'll take you back. Look out—here comes a basket. It's one of Dame Washalot's biggest ones. I borrowed it from her to go back in. All right, red squirrel, don't take my cushion. I'll put it in the basket to sit on.'

The red squirrel said goodbye and popped back into his hole. Moon-Face caught the big basket that came swinging down on a stout rope and threw his yellow cushion into it. He helped Connie in, tugged at the rope, and then up they swung between the branches of the tree. Up and up and up—past the Angry Pixie's, past the Owl's home, past Mister Watzisname, still snoring, past Dame Washalot, and right up to Moon-Face's house.

'Here we are!' he called to Joe and the Saucepan Man, who were busy tugging at the rope, to bring up the basket. 'Thanks so much.'

Everyone was amused to see that the bottom part of poor Connie's dress was gone. 'She's ragged now as

'*Look at my dress.*'

well as dirty,' said Saucepan, sounding quite pleased. He didn't like Connie. 'I wonder what will happen to her next.'

'Nothing, I hope,' said Connie, scowling at him.

'Soap? Yes, you do look as if you want a bit of soap,' said Saucepan, mis-hearing as usual. 'And a needle and thread too.'

'Now, stop it, Saucepan!' said Silky. 'I've never known you to be so quarrelsome. Come and eat the Hot-Cold Goodies. Nobody's had any yet.'

They went into Moon-Face's curved home, and sat down again. Connie tried not to go near the hole. She was very afraid of falling down it again. She took a Hot-Cold Goodie. It was like a very, very big chocolate.

Hot-Cold Goodies were mysterious. You put them into your mouth and sucked. As soon as you had sucked the chocolate part off, you came to what seemed like a layer of ice-cream.

'Oooh! Ice-cream!' said Joe, sucking hard. 'Cold as can be. Gosh, it's too cold to bear! It's getting colder and colder. Moon-Face, I'll have to spit out my goodie, it's too cold for me.'

But just as he said that the Hot-Cold Goodie stopped being cold and went hot. At first it was pleasantly warm, then it got very hot.

'It's almost burning me!' said Beth. 'Oh—now it's gone ice-cold again. Moon-Face, what extraordinary things. Wherever did you get them?'

'I bought them from a witch who popped down from the Land of Marvels today,' said Moon-Face, grinning. 'Funny, aren't they?'

Dinner with Moon-Face

'Yes—very exciting, and delicious to taste, once you get used to them changing from cold to hot, and hot to cold,' said Beth. 'I'll have another one.'

'What land did you say was at the top of the Tree today?' asked Silky. 'The Land of Marvels? Oh yes—I went there last year, I remember.'

'What was it like?' asked Frannie.

'Marvellous,' said Silky. 'All wonders and marvels. There's a ladder that hasn't any top—you go on and on climbing up it, and you never reach the top—and a tree that sings whenever the wind blows—a cat that tells your fortune—and a silver ball that takes you all round the world and back in the wink of an eye—well, I can't tell you all the marvels there are.'

'I'd like to go and see them,' said Joe.

'You can't,' said Silky. 'The land moves on today. It would be dangerous to go there now because it might move on at any moment. Then you'd be stuck in the Land of Marvels.'

'I don't believe a word of it,' said Connie.

'She doesn't believe in anything magic,' explained Joe, seeing that Silky looked rather surprised. 'Don't take any notice of her, Silky. She'll believe all right soon.'

'I will not,' said Connie. 'I'm beginning to think this is all a horrible dream.'

'Well, go home and go to bed and dream your dream there,' said Joe, getting tired of Connie.

'I will,' said Connie, getting up, offended. 'I'll climb down the Tree myself, and ask that kind red squirrel to see me home. This is a horrible party.'

27

The silly girl went to the door, opened it, went out and banged it shut. The others stared at one another.

'Is she always like that?' asked Moon-Face.

'Yes,' said Joe. 'She's a very spoilt child, you know. Wants her own way always, and turns up her nose at everything. I'd better fetch her back.'

'No, don't,' said Moon-Face. 'She can't come to any harm. Let her climb down the Tree if she wants to. I only hope she peeps in at the Angry Pixie's again. When I went past in the basket he was writing a letter again, but with red ink this time.'

'Then Connie will probably get red spots on her dress now!' said Frannie.

But Connie hadn't gone down the Tree. She stood outside on a branch, sulking. She looked down the Tree and saw Dame Washalot busy washing again. Silly old woman! Connie didn't feel as if she wanted to go near her, in case she got water all over her again. She looked upwards.

She was nearly at the top of the Tree. She thought it would be fun to climb right up to the top, and look down on the Enchanted Wood. What a long way she would see!

She climbed upwards. She came to the top of the Tree—and to her great astonishment the last branch of all touched the clouds! Yes—it went straight up into a vast white cloud that hung, floating, over the top of the Tree.

'Strange,' said Connie, looking up into the purple hole made by the tree branch in the cloud. 'Shall I go up there—into the cloud? Yes—I will.'

She went up the last branch—and there was a little ladder leading through the thickness of the cloud from the branch. A ladder!

Connie was filled with curiosity. She could hardly bear waiting to see what was at the top of the ladder. She climbed it—and suddenly her head poked right through the cloud, and into a new and different land altogether!

'Well!' said Connie, in surprise. 'So the children told the truth. There is a land at the top of the Faraway Tree—or am I really dreaming?'

She climbed up into the land. It was peculiar. There was a strange humming noise in the air. Strange people walked quickly past, some looking like witches, and some like goblins. They took no notice of Connie.

'The land is moving on!' cried one goblin to another. 'It's on the move again. Where shall we go to next?'

And then the Land of Marvels moved away from the top of the tree—and took poor Connie with it!

Off to Jack-and-the-Beanstalk

Joe, Beth, Frannie and the others went on with their meal. They finished the Hot-Cold Goodies, then they started on some pink desserts that Moon-Face had made in the shape of animals. They were so nicely made that it seemed a pity to eat them.

'We'd better save some for Connie, hadn't we?' said Beth. 'Let's see if she's outside the door. I expect she's standing there, sulking.'

Moon-Face opened the door. There was no one there. He called loudly, 'Connie! Connie!'

There was no answer. 'She's gone down the Tree, I should think,' he said. 'I'll just call down to Dame Washalot and see if she saw her.'

So he shouted down to the old dame. But Dame Washalot shook her head. 'No,' she shouted back, 'no one has gone past since you came up in the basket, Moon-Face. No one at all.'

'Funny!' said Moon-Face, going to tell the others. 'Where's she gone, then?'

'Up through the cloud?' said Silky.

'No—surely she wouldn't have done that by herself,' said Joe, in alarm. 'Look, Moon-Face! There's the red squirrel who wants to speak to you.'

The red squirrel came in, trying to hide a hole in his old sweater. 'I heard you calling Connie, Moon-Face,' he said. 'Well, she's gone up the ladder through the cloud. I expect she's in the Land of Marvels. I saw her go.'

'Good heavens!' cried Joe, jumping up in alarm. 'Why, the land is ready to leave here at any minute, didn't you say, Silky? What a silly she is! We'd better go and get her back at once.'

'I thought I heard the humming noise that means any land is moving on,' said Moon-Face, looking troubled. 'I don't believe we can save her. I'll run up the ladder and see.'

He climbed up the highest branch and went up the ladder. But there was nothing to be seen at all except swirling, misty cloud. He came down again.

'The Land of Marvels is gone,' he said. 'And the next land hasn't even come yet. I don't know what it will be, either. Well—Connie's gone with the Land of Marvels. She would do a silly thing like that!'

Beth went pale. 'But what can we do about it?' she said. 'Whatever can we do? We're in charge of her, you know. We really can't let her go like this. We must find her somehow.'

'How can we?' said Silky. 'You know that once a land has moved on, it doesn't come back for ages. Connie will have to stay there. It might do her good to be there for a while, anyway. She's not a very nice person.'

'Oh Silky, you don't understand!' said Joe. He looked very worried. 'She's our friend. And although she's silly and annoying at times, we're responsible and have to look after her and help her. How can we get to her?'

'You can't,' said Moon-Face.

Saucepan had been trying to follow what had been said, and he looked very concerned. He didn't like Connie, and he thought it was a very good thing she had gone off in the Land of Marvels. But he did know a way of getting there, and he badly wanted to tell the others.

But they all talked at once, and he couldn't get a word in! So, in despair he clashed his saucepans and kettles together so violently that everyone jumped and stared round at him.

'He wants to say something,' said Joe. 'Go on, out with it, Saucepan.'

Saucepan came out with it in a rush. 'I know how to get to the Land of Marvels without waiting for it to arrive here again,' he said. 'You can get to it from the Land of Giants, which joins on to it.'

'Well, I don't see how that helps us,' said Moon-Face. 'We don't know how to get to the Land of Giants either, silly!'

'No, it's not hilly,' said Saucepan, going all deaf again. 'It's quite flat. The giants have made it flat by walking about on it with their enormous feet.'

'What is he talking about?' said Beth. 'Saucepan, stop talking about the geography of Giantland and tell us how to get there.'

'How to get there, did you say?' asked Saucepan, putting his hand behind his left ear.

'YES!' yelled everyone.

'Well, that's easy,' said Saucepan, beaming round.

'Same way as Jack-and-the-Bean-Stalk did, of course. Up the Bean-Stalk!'

Everyone stared at Saucepan in silence. They had all heard of Jack-and-the-Bean-Stalk, of course, and how he climbed up the Bean-Stalk into Giantland.

'But where's the Bean-Stalk?' asked Joe at last.

'Where Jack lives,' said Saucepan, suddenly hearing well again. 'I know him quite well. Married a princess and lives in a castle.'

'I never knew that he was an old friend of yours,' said Moon-Face. 'How did you come to know him?'

'I sold him a lot of saucepans and kettles,' said the Saucepan Man. 'He was giving an enormous dinner party, and they didn't have enough things to cook everything in. So I came along just at the right moment and sold him everything I'd got. Very lucky for him.'

'And for you too,' grinned Moon-Face. 'Well, you'd better take us to your Jack, Saucepan. We'll go up the Bean-Stalk, and try and rescue that silly little Connie.'

'We'd better not all go,' said Joe, looking round at the little company.

'I must go to show you the way,' said Saucepan, who loved making a journey.

'And I must go, of course,' said Moon-Face.

'And I shall come with you to look after you,' said Silky, firmly. 'You always get into such silly scrapes if I'm not there to see to you.'

'And I shall certainly come, because I was really in charge of Connie,' said Joe.

'And we're not going to be left out of an adventure like this!' said Beth at once. 'Are we Frannie?'

33

'Well—it looks as if we're all going then,' said Moon-Face. 'All right, let's go. But don't let's get caught by any giants, for goodness' sake. Must we go through Giant-land to get to the Land of Marvels, Saucepan?'

'Must,' said Saucepan, cheerfully. 'The giants won't hurt you. They're quite harmless nowadays. Well, come on! Down the Tree we go, and then to the other end of the Wood.'

So down the Tree they went, and the red squirrel bounded with them to the bottom. They wished they could skip down as he did—it didn't take him more than half a minute to get up or down!

They reached the bottom, and then thought how silly they were not to have gone down the slippery-slip!

'It shows how worried we are, not to have thought of that!' said Beth. 'Which way now, Saucepan?'

Saucepan set off down a narrow, winding path. 'This way, look—under this bush, and across this field. We've got to get to the station,' he said.

'Station? What station?' said Joe, in astonishment.

'To get the train for Jack-and-the-Bean-Stalk's castle,' said Saucepan. 'How stupid you are, all of a sudden, Joe!'

They suddenly came to a small station set under a row of tall trees. A steam train came puffing in, looking very like an old wooden toy one that the children had at home. They got in, and it went off, puffing hard as if it was out of breath.

They passed through many mysterious little stations, but didn't stop. 'I said "Bean-Stalk Castle" to the engine, so it will go straight there,' said Saucepan.

34

The other passengers didn't seem to mind going to Bean-Stalk Castle at all. They sat and talked or read, and took no notice of the new little group of friends.

The train suddenly stopped and hooted. 'Here we are,' said Saucepan. 'Come on, everyone.'

They got out. The engine gave another hoot and went rattling off.

'There's Jack! Hi there, Jack!' yelled Saucepan, and rushed towards a sturdy young man in the distance. They shook hands, all Saucepan's kettles and pans rattling excitedly.

'What a pleasure, what a pleasure!' cried Jack. 'Who are all these people? Have they come to stay with me? I'll go and tell the Princess to make up extra beds at once.'

'No, don't do that,' said Moon-Face. 'We haven't come to stay. We just want to know—can we please use your Bean-Stalk, Jack?'

'It hasn't grown this year yet,' said Jack. 'I forgot to plant any beans, you see. And, the giants were a bit of a nuisance last year, always shouting rude things down the Bean-Stalk to me.'

'Oh!' said Joe, staring at Jack in dismay. 'What a pity! We particularly wanted to go up your Bean-Stalk.'

'Well—I can plant the beans now, and they'll grow,' said Jack. 'They're magic ones, you know. They grow as you watch them.'

'Oh, good!' said Moon-Face. 'Could you plant some, do you think? We'd be very grateful to you.'

'Certainly,' said Jack, and he felt about in his pocket. 'I'd do anything to help old Saucepan. His kettles and

35

saucepans are still going strong in my kitchen—never wear out at all. Now—wherever did I put those beans?'

The others watched anxiously as he turned an odd collection of things out of his pockets. At last came three or four mouldy-looking beans.

'Here we are,' said Jack. 'I'll just press them into the ground—like this—and now we'll watch them grow. Stand back, please, because they sometimes shoot up very fast!'

To the Land of Giants

Everyone watched the ground where Jack had buried the beans. At first nothing happened. Then a sort of little hill came, as if a mole was working there. The hill split and up came some Bean-Stalks, putting out two bean-leaves. Then other leaves sprang from the centre of the stalk, and pointed upwards. Then others came, and the Bean-Stalks grew higher and higher.

'Incredible!' said Beth, watching them grow up and up. 'They don't even need a pole to climb up, Jack. Is that how they grew when you first planted them, years ago, to climb up to Giantland?'

'Just the same,' said Jack. 'Look—you can't even see the tops of them now! It's amazing how they spring up, isn't it? Look how thick and strong the stems have grown, too!'

So they had. They were like the trunks of young trees.

'Have they reached Giantland yet?' asked Moon-Face squinting up.

'Can't tell till you climb up,' said Jack. 'I'd come with you, but I've got visitors coming—and the Princess isn't pleased if I'm not there to greet them. So I'd better go now.'

He shook hands politely all round, and was very pleased when the Saucepan Man presented him with an extra large kettle in return for his kindness. Beth was glad to see him taking the kettle.

Up the Bean-Stalk they all went. It was not at all difficult, for there were plenty of strong leaf-stalks to tread on and to haul themselves up by. But it did seem a very, very long way to the top!

'I think we're going to the Moon!' said Joe, panting. 'We'll see the Man in the Moon peeping at us over the top!'

But they didn't go to the Moon. They went to Giant-land, of course, because the beans never grew up to anywhere else. The topmost shoots waved over Giant-land, and the children and the others rolled off them and lay panting on the ground to rest.

'Phew! I couldn't have climbed any further!' said Beth, trying to get her breath. 'Oh my, what ever is that, Joe?'

'It's an earthquake!' cried Frannie. 'Can't you feel the earth trembling and quaking?'

'Here's a mountain coming on top of us!' shouted Joe, and pulled Beth and Frannie down a nearby hole.

Saucepan peered down, laughing. 'No earthquake and no mountain!' he said. 'Just an ordinary giant coming along, whose footsteps shake the ground.'

The noise and the earthquake grew worse and then passed. The giant had gone by. Everyone breathed again and crept out of the hole.

'I suppose that's a rabbit hole we were in, where giant rabbits live,' said Beth.

'No—a worm hole, where giant worms live,' said Moon-Face. 'I saw one down at the bottom, like an enormous snake.'

'Oh dear—I won't go down a hole like that again!' said Frannie. But she did, when another earthquake and walking mountain appeared! It was another giant, tall as the sky, his great feet shaking the earth below.

'Come on!' said Moon-Face, when the second giant had gone safely by. 'We must hurry. And for goodness' sake get out of the way if another giant comes by, because we don't want to be squashed like raisins under his feet.'

The third giant stopped when he came near them. He bent down, and the children saw that he wore glasses on his enormous nose. They looked as large as shop windows!

'Ha! What are these little creatures?' said the giant, in a voice that boomed like a thunder storm. 'Beetles, I should think—or ants! Most extraordinary, I have never seen any like them before!'

There was no hole to slip down. The children saw that the giant was trying to pick one of them up! An enormous hand, with fingers as thick as young tree trunks came down near them.

Everyone was too scared to move, and there was nowhere to hide, except for a large dandelion growing as tall as a tree, nearby. But Saucepan had a bright idea. He undid his biggest saucepan, and clapped it on top of the giant's thumb; it fitted it exactly, and stuck there.

The giant gave a loud cry of surprise, and lifted up

his hand. He stood up to see this funny thing that had suddenly appeared on his thumb, and Saucepan yelled to everyone.

'To the dandelion, quick! Hurry!'

They rushed to the tall dandelion plant. One of the heads floated high above them, a beautiful ripe dandelion 'clock', full of seeds ready to fly off in the wind.

Saucepan shook the stalk violently, and some of the seeds flew off, floating in the air on their parachute of hairs.

'Catch the stalks of the seeds, catch them, and let the wind float you away!' yelled Saucepan. 'The giant won't guess we're flying off with the dandelion seeds.'

So each of them caught hold of a dandelion seed. Frannie got two, and held on tightly! Then the wind blew, and the plumy seeds floated high in the air, taking everyone with them. They saw the giant kneel down on the ground to look for the funny creatures that had put the saucepan on his thumb—but then they were off and away, floating high in the breeze.

'Keep together, keep together!' called Moon-Face, grabbing Silky's hand. 'We don't want to be blown apart, all over Giantland. We'd never meet again! Hold hands when you get near.'

Frannie was nearly lost, because she had hold of two seeds instead of one, and was blown higher than the others. But Joe managed to grab her feet and pulled her down beside him. He made her leave go of one of her dandelion seeds, and took hold of her hand firmly.

Now they were all linking hands in pairs, and kept together well. They floated high over Giantland, marvelling at the enormous castles there, the great gardens and tall trees.

'Even the Faraway Tree would look small here!' said Beth.

'Look—there's the boundary between the Land of Marvels and Giantland!' cried Saucepan suddenly, almost letting go of his dandelion seed in his excitement. 'I'd no idea we would get there so soon. What a wall!'

It was indeed a marvellous wall. It rose steadily up, so high that it seemed to have no end, and it shimmered and shook as if it was made of water.

'It's a magic wall,' said Saucepan. 'I remember seeing it before. No giant can get in or out, over or under it, because it's painted with giant-proof paint.'

'What's that?' asked Joe, shouting.

'Giant-proof paint can only be bought in the Land of Marvels,' explained Saucepan. 'Anything painted with it keeps giants away, just like the smell of camphor keeps moths away. It's marvellous. No giant can come close to anything painted with that silvery magic paint. I only wish I had some!'

'Well—how are we to get over or under this wall?' said Moon-Face, as they floated near. 'It may be giant-proof, but it looks as if it's us-proof too!'

'Oh no—we can go right through it,' said Silky. 'You'll see that as soon as we get right up to it, it won't be there! It's only giant-proof.'

This sounded impossible, but Silky's words were quite true. When they reached the wall, it gave one last shimmer—and was gone! The children floated right down into the Land of Marvels, where everything was the right size. It was a great relief to see things properly again, and not to have to crane your neck to see if a flower was a daisy or a pimpernel!

They floated to the ground, let go of their dandelion seeds, which gradually became the right size, once they were away from Giantland, and looked round them.

'There's the ladder-without-a-top,' said Silky, pointing. 'No one has ever climbed beyond the three thousandth rung, because they get so tired. And there's the tree-that-sings. It's singing now.'

So it was—a whispery, beautiful song, all about the sun and the wind and rain. The children could understand it perfectly, although the tree did not use any words they knew. It just stood there and poured out its song in tree language.

'I could listen to that for ages,' said Joe. 'But we really must get on. Now—we must all hunt for Connie. Let's shout for her, shall we? Now—altogether—shout!'

They shouted. 'CON-NEE! CON-NEE! CON-NEE!'

An old woman nearby looked angrily at them. 'Be quiet!' she said. 'Making such a noise! I've a good mind to change you all into a thunder storm. Then you can make as much noise as you like! It's bad enough to have one child here, making a fuss and yelling and screaming, without having a whole crowd!'

'Oh—have you seen a child here?' said Joe, at once. 'Where is she, please? We are looking for her.'

'She went up the ladder-that-has-no-top,' said the

old woman. 'And she hasn't come down. I hope she stays up there for ever!'

'Oh—bother Connie!' groaned Joe. 'Now we'll have to do a bit more climbing, and see how far up the ladder she's gone! Come on!'

So off they all went to the shining ladder, that stretched from the ground up and up and up. No top could be seen.

'I'll go,' said Moon-Face. 'I'm not tired, and all of you are. I'll bring Connie down. I doubt if she's gone further than the hundredth rung!'

He went up the ladder, and the others sat down at the bottom waiting. They waited and they waited. Why didn't Moon-Face come back?

Up the Ladder-That-Has-No-Top

Joe and the others waited and waited, looking up the ladder every now and again. Beth got impatient and wandered off to look at some of the marvels. Joe called her back.

'Beth! Don't go wandering off by yourself, for goodness' sake! We don't want to lose you, as soon as we find Connie. We'll have a look at the marvels when Moon-Face brings Connie back.'

'Well, he's such a long time up the ladder,' complained Beth. 'I did want to go and see the cat-that-tells-fortunes. She might tell me how we can get back home!'

'Back through Giantland, I suppose?' said Silky.

'I wish Moon-Face would come!' sighed Frannie, looking up the ladder for the twentieth time. 'What is he doing up there? Surely Connie can't have climbed very far!'

Moon-Face had gone up a good way. He climbed steadily, looking up every now and again, hoping to see Connie. At last he saw a pair of feet, and he gave a yell.

'Connie! I've come to rescue you! It's Moon-Face coming up the ladder!'

The feet didn't move. They were big feet, and it suddenly struck Moon-Face that they were too big to be Connie's. He looked above the feet, and saw a goblin looking down at him.

'Oh!' said Moon-Face. 'I thought you were Connie. Let me pass, please.'

'Can't think why there's so much traffic on this ladder today,' said the goblin, grumbling as he sat to one side. He had big feet, big hands, a big head, and a very small body, so he looked rather odd. On his knees he balanced a big can of paint, out of which stuck a paint brush.

'What are you doing up here?' asked Moon-Face. 'Painting or something?'

'I'm the goblin painter who made that wall giant-proof,' said the goblin. He pointed to where the wall between Giantland and the Land of Marvels shimmered and quivered like a heat-haze. 'But I got into trouble with Witch Wily, who used to go and shop in Giantland. I splashed some of my paint over her, and that meant she was giant-proof too. No giant in Giantland could go near her, so she couldn't do any more shopping!'

'So she chased you, I suppose, to put a spell on you, and you rushed up the ladder-that-has-no-top!' said Moon-Face, sitting down beside him to peer at his paint. 'Bad luck! Why doesn't she chase you up here?'

'She doesn't like climbing,' said the goblin. 'But she's waiting down there at the bottom, I'm sure of it.'

'She isn't,' said Moon-Face. 'I've just come up, and there was no witch down there. You go on down now, and see. I'm sure you can slip off and escape.'

'She said she'd empty my giant-proof paint all over me if she caught me,' said the goblin, miserably.

'Well, leave it here with me,' said Moon-Face. 'I'll bring it down for you. Then, if the witch is at the bottom it won't matter, because you won't have your paint with you.'

'Right!' said the goblin, cheering up. He tied the handle of his paint can to a rung of the ladder, and began to go down. Moon-Face suddenly remembered Connie, and he called down to the goblin.

'Hey! Just a minute! Have you seen a little girl go up the ladder?'

'Oh yes,' said the goblin, stopping. 'A dirty little girl, very frightened. She was crying. She pushed past me very rudely indeed. I didn't like her.'

'Oh, that's Connie all right,' said Moon-Face, and he began to climb up again. 'I hope she hasn't gone too far up. She really is a nuisance.'

He lost sight of the goblin. He went on climbing up and up, and at last he heard a miserable voice above him. It was Connie's.

'I can't climb any further! This ladder doesn't lead anywhere. I can't climb down because that goblin will scold me. I shall have to stay here for the rest of my life. Boo-hoo, boo-hoo!'

Connie sobbed, and two or three tears splashed down on Moon-Face's head. He rubbed them off. Then he saw Connie's feet above him.

'Hey, Connie!' he called.

Connie gave a shriek and almost fell off the ladder. Moon-Face felt it wobbling. 'Oh! Oh! Who is it?' cried

Connie, and began to climb hurriedly up the ladder again, afraid that the goblin was after her.

This was too much for Moon-Face. Here he was, having gone all the way to the Land of Marvels, through Giantland, and up goodness knows how many rungs of the ladder—and just as he had found Connie she began climbing up and up again. He caught firmly hold of one of her ankles. She screamed.

'Let go! I'll pinch you! Let go!'

'You come down,' commanded Moon-Face. 'I've come to take you back home, you silly girl. You've caused us all a lot of trouble. Come on down! I'm Moon-Face.'

Connie sat down on the ladder with great relief. She put her arms round Moon-Face as he came up beside her, and hugged him.

'Moon-Face! I was never so pleased to see anyone. Tell me how you got here.'

'No,' said Moon-Face, wriggling away. 'There's no time. The others are waiting at the foot of the ladder. Come on down, you silly girl!'

'But there's a gob . . .' began Connie.

'No, there isn't,' said Moon-Face, beginning to wonder how many other people there were sitting on the ladder, afraid to go down because they thought someone was watching for them at the bottom. 'There's no goblin and no witch and no nothing. Only Joe, Beth, Frannie, Silky and Saucepan. Come on, please!'

He made Connie climb down below him. 'Now, if you don't climb down pretty fast, I shall be treading on your fingers!' he said, and that made Connie climb

47

down much more quickly than she had meant to. Down and down they went, down and down. And, at last, there they were on the ground!

The others crowded round them. 'Moon-Face! We thought you were never coming!'

'Connie! Are you all right?'

'A goblin came hurrying down, but he wouldn't stop to tell us anything!'

'Moon-Face, what have you got in that can?'

Moon-Face showed them the can of giant-proof paint he had brought down with him. He had untied it from the ladder when he came to it. He told them about the goblin.

Connie was longing to tell her adventures, too. She told them at last.

'When I got here, into this land, I wandered about a bit,' she said. 'And I came to the cat that could tell fortunes, so I asked her to tell me mine. And she told me all kinds of nasty things that would happen to me, so I scolded her, and she hissed and ran away.'

'You naughty girl!' said Silky.

'Well, she shouldn't have said nasty things to me,' said Connie. 'Then a goblin, whose cat it was, chased me and said he would lock me up. Horrid creature!'

The others laughed. They thought Connie deserved all she got.

'So I suppose you shot up the ladder to escape and didn't dare to come down?' said Joe.

'Yes,' said Connie. 'And I was so pleased to see Moon-Face. I don't like this land. And I don't like the Faraway Tree either, or the Enchanted Wood.'

'Or me, or Beth, or Frannie, or Silky, or Moon-Face, or Saucepan, I suppose?' said Joe. 'Pleasant child, aren't you? I think if I was a goblin I would certainly chase you away. Well, what about going home? It's getting late.'

'Oh dear—have we got to go through Giantland again?' said Silky. 'I didn't like those enormous giants. I'm afraid of their great big feet.'

'Yes, we've got to go through Giantland,' said Moon-Face. 'But I've got an idea. I'll splash you all with a few drops of giant-proof paint! Then no giant can come near us. We'll be like that wall—giant-proof!'

'Oh, what a good idea!' said Beth. So Moon-Face quickly dabbed a few drops of paint on each of them. The places he dabbed shone and shimmered strangely, like the wall. The children laughed.

'We look peculiar. Never mind—if it keeps the giants away from us, it will be worth it.'

They made their way to the shining wall, which disappeared as they walked through it, and re-appeared again as soon as they were on the other side. Then they began to walk cautiously through Giantland, to find the top of the Bean-Stalk.

Many giants were out, taking an evening walk. Some of them saw the children and pointed in surprise. They knelt down to pick them up.

But they couldn't touch them! The giant-proof paint prevented any giant from getting too near, and no matter how they tried they couldn't get hold of any of the little group of friends.

'This is jolly good stuff, this paint,' said Joe, pleased. 'It was a good idea of yours, Moon-Face.'

'Look—there's the top of the Bean-Stalk,' said Silky, happily. 'Now we won't be long!'

The giants followed them to the Bean-Stalk. The children and the others climbed down as quickly as they could, half afraid that the giants might shake the Bean-Stalk so that they would fall off. But they didn't. They just called rudely down after them. They got to the ground and sighed with relief.

'My goodness, we're late!' said Joe, looking at his watch. 'We must head for home at once. Where's that train?'

Soon they were in the funny little train. They got out at the Enchanted Wood, said goodbye to Moon-Face, Silky and Saucepan, and made their way home. Connie was very tired.

'Well—I guess you didn't enjoy the party very much?' said Joe to Connie. 'And what about the Faraway Tree and the people there? Do you believe in them now?'

'I suppose I'll have to,' said Connie. 'But I didn't like any of them much, except Moon-Face. I can't bear Saucepan.'

'He doesn't seem to like you, either,' said Beth. 'Well, Connie—you don't need to come with us again if you don't want to. We can leave you behind.'

But that didn't please Connie! No—she meant to go where the others went. She wasn't going to be left out!

The Faraway Tree Again

Mother wasn't very pleased to see how dirty, ink-stained and ragged Connie's clothes were when she came back with the others.

'I won't let you go with the others to the Faraway Tree again if you can't keep youself cleaner than this,' she said, crossly. Connie was not used to being talked to like this, and she burst into tears.

The children's mother popped Connie's clothes into the washtub and said, 'Tomorrow you will iron and mend these clothes, Connie. Stop that noise, or I will send you to bed straight away.'

All the children were tired, and fell asleep as soon as their heads touched the pillow. When Connie woke up, she remembered all that had happened the day before, and wondered if she could possibly have dreamt it. It seemed so amazing when she thought about it.

'Are we going to the Faraway Tree today again?' she asked Joe, when they were all having breakfast.

Joe shook his head.

'No, We've got lots of work to do. And anyway you didn't like it, or the people there, so we'll go alone.'

Connie looked as if she was going to burst into tears. Then she remembered that tears didn't seem to bother anyone here, so she blinked them away. 'What land will be at the top of the tree this week?' she asked.

'Don't know,' said Joe. 'Anyway, we're not going, Connie. We've had enough travelling this week!'

For the next two days it rained so hard that Mother wouldn't let the children go out. They heard nothing from their friends in the Faraway Tree.

The next day was sunny and the sky was a lovely blue. 'As if it had been washed clean by all the rain,' said Frannie. 'Let's go to the Enchanted Wood. Can we, Mother?'

'Well, yes, I should think so,' said Mother. 'I badly want a new saucepan, a nice little one for boiling milk. You could go and ask the Saucepan Man to sell me one. Here's some money.'

'Oh, lovely!' said Beth, overjoyed at the thought of visiting the Faraway Tree folk again. 'We'll go this morning.'

'I'm going too,' said Connie.

'You're not,' said Joe. 'You're going to stay at home like a good girl, and help Mother. You'll like that.'

'Indeed I won't!' said Connie. 'Don't be mean. Take me with you.'

'Well, it's no fun taking you anywhere,' said Joe. 'You've got bad manners, and you don't do what you're told, and people don't like you. You'll be far better at home. Anyway, you don't believe in anything in the Enchanted Wood, so why do you want to come?'

'Because I don't want to be left out,' wailed Connie. 'Let me come. I'll be good. I'll have nice manners. I'll like everyone.'

'Well, you won't go in that nice dress,' said Mother, firmly. 'I'm not going to let you spoil another one. If you go, you must borrow some old clothes of Frannie's. They're a bit patched, but that won't matter.'

Connie didn't want to wear Frannie's old clothes, but she went to put them on. She couldn't bear being left out, and if the others were going off to the Wood she really must go too. She came back wearing Frannie's old washed-out clothes.

'You look sensible now,' said Joe. 'Very sensible. It won't even matter if you go down the slippery-slip without a cushion again. That material won't wear out in a hurry. Come on, everybody!'

They set off, Joe jingling the money for the saucepan in his pocket. They jumped over the ditch and landed in the Enchanted Wood. At once everything seemed magic and different. Connie felt excited again. She was longing to see Moon-Face who, since he had rescued her from the Land of Marvels, had become her hero.

They came to the Faraway Tree. It was so hot that the children didn't feel like climbing up.

'We'll go up on cushions,' said Joe. 'We'll send the red squirrel up to tell Moon-Face to send some down on the ropes.'

He whistled a little tune and the red squirrel popped out of his hole. 'Your sweater is getting so holey you won't be able to keep it on soon!' said Beth.

'I know,' said the squirrel. 'But I don't know how to mend it.'

'I'll do it for you one day,' said Beth. 'I'm good at

53

needlework. Now, squirrel, please go up to Moon-Face and ask him to send down four cushions on ropes. It's really too hot to climb up today.'

The red squirrel bounded up the Tree as light as a feather, his plumy tail waving behind him. The children sat down and waited, watching the funny little folk that trotted up and down the big Tree, going about their business.

There soon came a rustling of leaves, and down through the branches came four fat cushions, tied firmly to ropes. 'Here we are,' said Joe, jumping up. 'Moon-Face has been jolly quick. Choose a cushion, Connie, and sit on it. Hold the rope tightly, give it three tugs, and up you'll go!'

It was exciting. Connie sat on the big, soft cushion, held on to the rope, and gave it three tugs. The rope was hauled up from above, and Connie went swinging upwards between the branches. She saw that the Tree was growing apricots that day. She wondered if they were ripe.

She picked one and it was deliciously sweet and juicy. She thought she would pick another one, but by that time the Tree was growing acorns, which was disappointing.

Soon everyone was on the broad branch outside Moon-Face's house. He was there with Mister Watzisname, pulling hard at the ropes.

'Hello!' said Mister Watzisname, beaming at the children. 'Haven't seen you for a long time.'

'You've always been asleep when we've come here,' said Joe. 'Watzisname, this is Connie.'

'Ah—how do you do?' said Watzisname. 'Is this the little girl Saucepan was telling me about? She doesn't look so dirty and ragged as he said.'

'Well!' began Connie, indignantly. 'Fancy Saucepan saying . . .'

'Now, don't lose your temper,' said Joe. 'After all, you did look dirty and ragged the other day. Where is Saucepan, Moon-Face? I want to buy something from him.'

'He's gone up into the land at the top of the Tree,' said Moon-Face. 'He heard that there was an old friend of his there, Little Miss Muffet, and he wanted to go and see her. She once gave him some curds and whey when he was very hungry, and he has never forgotten it. It was the only time in his life he ever tasted curds and whey.'

'Oh!' said Joe. 'Well, what land is up there this week, then?'

'The Land of Nursery Rhyme,' said Moon-Face. 'So Watzisname says, anyway. You went up, didn't you Watzisname, and saw Little Tommy Tucker, and Little Jack Horner?'

'Yes,' said Watzisname. 'Quite an interesting land. All sorts of friendly people there.'

'Let's go up and find Saucepan!' said Beth. 'It will be fun. It's quite a harmless land, that's obvious. Goodness knows how long Saucepan will be up there with Little Miss Muffet. Maybe he's feasting on curds and whey again, and won't be back for days!'

'Oh—please let's go!' said Connie. 'And Moon-Face, dear Moon-Face, you come too.'

'Don't call me 'Dear Moon-Face',' said Moon-Face. 'You're not my best friend yet.'

'Oh!' said Connie, who was so used to being fussed and spoilt by everyone that she couldn't understand anybody not liking her.

'I think it would be fun to go up and see the Nursery Rhyme people,' said Joe. 'Come on—let's go now. We could get a saucepan from the Old Saucepan Man while we're there, and take it back with us.'

'Well, come along, then,' said Moon-Face, and he led the way up the topmost branch of the Tree. One by one they climbed it, came to the little ladder that led through the cloud, and found themselves in yet another land.

'The Land of Nursery Rhyme!' said Beth, looking round. 'Well—we should know most of the people here, though they won't know us! I wonder where Saucepan is. He could introduce us to everyone.'

'We'll ask where Little Miss Muffet lives,' said Moon-Face. 'Look—that must be Jack Horner, over there, carrying a pie!'

'Ask him where Miss Muffet is,' said Frannie.

So they went over to where a plump little boy was just about to make a hole in his pie with his thumb.

'Please, where is Miss Muffet?' asked Joe.

'Over the other side of the hill,' said Jack Horner, pointing with a juicy thumb. 'Look out for her spider— he's pretty fierce today!'

Nursery Rhyme Land

'What did he mean—look out for the spider?' asked Connie, looking round worriedly.

'Well, you know that a spider keeps coming and sitting down beside Miss Muffet whenever she eats her curds and whey, don't you?' said Joe. 'We've just got to look out for it.'

'I'm scared of spiders,' said Connie, looking as if she was going to cry.

'You would be!' said Joe. 'You're just the kind of person who's afraid of bats and moths and spiders and everything. Don't be silly. Go back if you'd rather not come with us.'

'All the same—it may be quite a big spider,' said Frannie.

Connie looked even more alarmed.

The children, Moon-Face and Watzisname walked to the hill, went up it, and stood at the top. Nursery Rhyme Land was nice. Its houses and cottages had thatched roofs, and the little gardens were full of flowers. The children felt that they knew everyone they met.

'Here's Tommy Tucker!' whispered Frannie, as a little boy hurried by, singing loudly in a clear, sweet voice. He heard her whisper and turned.

'Do you know me?' he asked in surprise. 'I don't know you.'

'Are you Tommy Tucker?' asked Beth. 'Were you going to sing for your supper?'

'Of course not. It's morning,' said Tommy. 'I sing for my supper at night. I was just practising a bit then. Do you sing for your supper?'

'No, We just have it, without singing,' said Joe.

'You're lucky,' said Tommy. 'Nobody will give me any if I don't sing. It's a good thing I've got a nice voice!'

He went off singing like a blackbird again. The others watched him, and then saw someone else coming along crying bitterly. A small boy was walking along, while a bigger boy was giving him a scolding. Behind the two came a thin cat, its fur wet and draggled.

'Hey! Stop scolding that little boy!' cried Joe, who didn't like to see a small boy being bullied by a bigger one. 'Pick someone your own size!'

'Mind your own business,' said the big boy. 'Johnny Thin deserves all he gets. You don't know what a bad boy he is!'

'Johnny Thin! Oh, isn't he the boy who put the cat down the well?' cried Frannie. 'Then you must be Johnny Stout, who pulled her out!'

'Yes—and there's the cat, poor thing,' said Johnny Stout. 'Now don't you think that bad boy deserves a good scolding?'

'Oh yes,' said Beth. 'He does. Poor cat. I'll dry it a bit.'

She got out her handkerchief and tried to dry the cat. But it was too wet.

58

'Don't bother,' said Johnny Stout, giving Johnny Thin a final scolding that sent him off howling loudly. 'I'll take the cat to Polly Flinders. She's always sitting by a fire, warming her toes!'

He picked up the cat and went into a nearby cottage. The children went and peeped in at the open door. They saw a little girl in the room inside, sitting close to a roaring fire, her toes wriggling in the heat.

Johnny Stout gave the cat to the little girl. 'Here you are, Polly!' he said. 'Dry her a bit, will you? She got put down the well again. But I've given Johnny Thin a good scolding, so maybe he won't do it any more.'

Polly Flinders took the cat on her lap, which made her pretty dress all wet. Johnny Stout was just going out of the door when somebody else came in. It was Polly Flinders' mother. When she saw Polly sitting among the cinders, warming her toes and nursing the wet cat, she gave an angry cry.

'You naughty little girl! How many times have I told you not to sit so close to the fire? What's the good of dressing you up in nice clothes if you make them so dirty? I'll teach you to be good!'

The children, Moon-Face and Watzisname felt rather scared of the angry mother. Johnny Stout ran away and the others thought it would be better to go too.

They went down the other side of the hill.

'Hello—who are these two coming up the hill?' said Moon-Face.

'Jack and Jill, of course!' said Beth. And so it was, carrying a pail between them. They filled it at the well

59

that stood at the top of the hill, and then began to go carefully down the hill.

'Oh—I do hope they don't fall down,' said Frannie, anxiously. 'They always do, in the rhyme!'

Jack and Jill began to quarrel as they went down the hill. 'Don't go so fast, Jack!' shouted Jill.

'You're always so slow!' grumbled Jack. 'Do hurry up!'

'The pail's so heavy!' cried Jill, and began to lag behind just as they came to a steep bit.

'They'll fall down—and Jack will break his crown again—he'll hurt his head badly!' said Beth. 'I'm going to stop them!'

She ran to the two children, who stopped, surprised. 'Don't quarrel, Jack and Jill,' begged Beth. 'You know you'll only fall down and hurt yourselves. Jill, let me take the handle of the pail. I can go as fast as Jack likes. Then for once you will get to the bottom of the hill safely, without falling down.'

Jill let go of the pail handle. Beth took it. Jack smiled at her. 'Thank you,' he said. 'Jill's always so slow. Come along with me, and I'll give you one of my toffees. I've got a whole bag full at home.'

Beth liked toffees. 'Oh, thank you,' she said. 'I'd like one.' She turned to the others. 'You go on to Miss Muffet's,' she said. 'I'll join you later.'

So off went the others, while Jack, Jill and Beth went down the hill together.

The others came to a gate with a name painted on it. 'LITTLE MISS MUFFET'.

'This is the place,' said Joe, pleased. 'Now we'll find

old Saucepan. Hey, Saucepan, are you anywhere about?'

The door was shut. No one came. Joe banged on the knocker. Rat-a-tat-tat! Still no one came.

'There's someone peeping out of the window,' said Moon-Face, suddenly. 'It looks like Miss Muffet.'

A little bit of blind had been pushed to one side, and a frightened eye, a little nose, and a curl could be seen. That was all.

'It is Miss Muffet!' said Watzisname. 'Miss Muffet, what's the matter? Why don't you open the door? Where is Saucepan?'

The blind fell back. There came a scamper of feet, and then the door opened a tiny bit. 'Come in, quickly, all of you—quick, quick, quick!'

Her voice was so scared that everyone felt frightened. They crowded into the cottage quickly.

'What's the matter?' asked Moon-Face. 'Has anything happened? Where's Saucepan? Didn't he come?'

'Yes, he came. But he was rude to my spider,' said Miss Muffet. 'He danced all round it, clashing his kettles and saucepans, and he sang a rude song, that began, "Two snaps for a spider . . ."'

'Just like Saucepan!' groaned Moon-Face. 'Well, what's happened?'

'The spider pounced on him and carried him off,' wept Miss Muffet. 'I brought him all the curds and whey in the house, but it didn't make any difference. He took no notice, and carried Saucepan away to his home. It's a sort of cave in the ground, with a web door. No one can get through it except the spider.'

'Well!' said Moon-Face, sitting down hard on a little chair. 'How very annoying! How are we going to get him out? Why must he go and annoy the spider like that?'

'Well, the spider came and suddenly sat down beside me, and made me jump,' said Miss Muffet. 'He's always doing that. It made me run away, and Saucepan said he would give the spider a fright to pay him back.'

'So he made up one of his silly songs, and did his crashing, clanging dance!' said Joe. 'What are we going to do? Do you think the spider will let Saucepan go?'

'Oh no—not till the Land of Nursery Rhyme moves on,' said Miss Muffet. 'He means to punish him well. I don't know if Saucepan will mind living here. He doesn't really belong, of course.'

'He'd hate to live here always and never see any of us except when the Land of Nursery Rhyme happened to come to the top of the Faraway Tree,' said Moon-Face. 'We must go and talk to that spider. Come on, all of you!'

'Oh—must I come?' asked Connie.

'Yes—the more of us that go, the better,' said Watzisname. 'The spider may feel afraid when he sees so many people marching up! You come too, Miss Muffet.'

So they all went, to face the spider in his webby cave. Connie and Miss Muffet walked hand in hand behind, ready to run! Neither of them was very brave.

'Beth will wonder where we are,' said Joe, remembering that she had gone off with Jack and Jill. 'Never mind—we'll find her when we've rescued Saucepan.'

They came to a cave in the ground. It had a thick, grey web door. From inside came a mournful voice:

> 'Two snaps for a spider,
> Two taps on his nose.
> Two claps on his ankles,
> Hi-tiddley-toze!'

'That's Saucepan, singing his rude spider song again,' whispered Miss Muffet. 'Oh—look out! There's the spider!'

Miss Muffet's Spider

'There's the spider! Here he comes!' cried everyone.

And the spider certainly was there. He was very large, had eight eyes to see with, and eight hairy legs to walk with. He wore a blue and red scarf round his neck, and he sneezed as he came.

'Wish-oo! Wish-oo! Bother this cold! No sooner do I lose one cold than I get another!'

He suddenly saw the little group of six people, and he stared with all his eight eyes. 'What do you want?' he said.

Moon-Face went forward boldly, looking far braver than he felt.

'We've come to tell you to set our friend free,' he said. 'Open that webby door at once and let him out. We know he's down there, because we can hear him singing.'

Out floated Saucepan's voice. 'Two snaps for a spider . . .'

'There! He's singing that rude song again!' said the spider, looking annoyed. 'No, I certainly won't let him go. He needs a lesson.'

'You must let him go!' said Moon-Face. 'He doesn't belong to your land. He belongs to ours. He'll be very unhappy here.'

'Serves him right,' said the spider. 'A wish-oo! A wish-oo! Bother this cold.'

'I hope you get hundreds of colds!' said Moon-Face, angrily. 'Are you going to let Saucepan free, or do we slash that door to bits?'

'Try if you like!' said the spider, taking out a big red handkerchief from somewhere. 'You'll be sorry, that's all I can say.'

'Anyone got a stick?' asked Moon-Face. Nobody had. So Moon-Face marched to a nearby bush and cut out two or three strong sticks. He gave one to Joe, one

Cutting strong sticks

to Watzisname, and another to Frannie. He could see that Connie and Miss Muffet wouldn't be much use, so he didn't give them one.

'Now—slash down the door!' cried Moon-Face.

The spider didn't say anything, but a horrid smile came on its face. It sat down and watched.

Moon-Face ran to the webby door and slashed at it with his stick. Joe and Watzisname slashed too, and Frannie followed.

But the webby door stuck to their sticks, and wound itself all round them. They tried to get it off, but the web stuck to them too. Soon it was floating about in long threads fastening itself round their legs and arms.

The spider got up. Connie and Miss Muffet were frightened and ran off as fast as they could. They hid under a bush and watched. They saw the spider push Joe, Moon-Face, Frannie and Watzisname into a heap together, and then roll them up in grey web so that they were caught like flies.

Then he bundled them all into his cave, and sat down to spin another webby door.

'A wish-oo!' sneezed the spider, suddenly. Then he coughed. He certainly had a terrible cold. He spied Connie and Miss Muffet under the bush and called to them.

'You come over here, too, and I'll wrap you up nice and cosy in my web!'

Both Connie and Miss Muffet squealed and ran back to Miss Muffet's cottage as fast as they could. When they got there they saw Beth coming along with Jack and Jill.

'Hello, Miss Muffet!' called Jack. 'Guess what, because of Beth's help, I got down the hill for the first time without falling over and hurting my head. Mother was very pleased, and she said we can have the whole day to play. So we thought we'd come and spend it with the other children, and Moon-Face. Where are they?'

'Oh, they've been taken prisoner by Miss Muffet's spider!' said Connie. She told them all about it, and Beth stared in horror. What! Joe and Frannie being kept prisoner by a horrid old spider! Whatever could be done?

'And he had an awful cold,' finished Connie. 'I never knew spiders could catch colds before. He was coughing and sneezing just like we do.'

'Sounds as if he ought to be in bed,' said Jill. 'Look out—here he comes!'

'A wish-oo!' said the spider, as he came by. 'A wish-oo! Bother this cold!'

'Why don't you do something for it?' said Jill, stepping boldly forward. She knew the spider quite well, and was not afraid of him.

'Well, I've put a scarf on, haven't I?' said the spider, sniffing. 'What more can I do?'

'You'd better put your feet in a mustard bath,' said Jack. 'That's what Mother makes us do if we have a bad cold. And we have to go to bed too, and drink hot lemon.'

'That does sound nice and comforting,' said the spider. 'But I've got no bed, and no one to look after me—and no lemon.'

'If Miss Muffet will lend you a bed, and squeeze you

67

a lemon, Jack and I will look after you,' said Jill. Miss Muffet stared at her in horror, but Jill gave her a nudge. She had a reason for saying all this. Miss Muffet swallowed hard and then nodded.

'All right! He can have my spare bed—but he is not to wander about my house and eat my curds and whey.'

'I won't, I promise I won't,' said the spider, gratefully. 'I'll be very good indeed. Thank you, Miss Muffet. Perhaps I won't frighten you any more after this.'

'What about a bath to put his feet in?' said Jill. 'You haven't got a big enough one, Miss Muffet. You see, a spider has eight feet, not two.'

'I've got a big bath in my cave,' said the spider. 'I'll go and get it.'

'Certainly not,' said Jack. 'You mustn't go about in the open air any more, with that dreadful cold. You get into bed at once. I'll fetch your bath.'

'But—but—there's a webby door over my cave— and you can't possibly get through it—and besides, there are prisoners there,' said the spider.

'Well, tell me how to undo the door without getting caught up in that nasty webby stuff,' said Jack. 'Then I can get your bath and bring it here.'

'Have you got a nice big cotton reel, Miss Muffet?' asked the spider. 'You have? Good! Give it to Jack and he can take it with him. You'll find the end thread of the webby door just by the handle, Jack. Take hold of it and pull. Wind it round the reel and the web will unravel nicely. You will be able to pull the door undone just like people pull a woollen sweater undone!'

'Well, I never!' said Jill, in surprise. 'That's something to know, anyway. Is that the reel, Miss Muffet? Right! We'll go. We'll leave you to see the spider into bed, and squeeze him a lemon, and put a kettle on to boil. Then, when we come back with the bath, we can put mustard and hot water into it, and make the spider put his feet in. Then his cold will soon be better.'

The spider looked very happy at being cared for like this. He looked gratefully at the children out of his eight eyes.

Connie, Jack and Jill and Beth set off. The spider called after them. 'Hey! What about my prisoners? I don't want them to escape. You'll find them all bound up in web. Leave them like that, and put a stone or something over the opening of my cave, will you?'

'We'll find a nice big stone,' promised Jack. 'Now hurry up and get into bed.'

Soon the four of them got to the spider's cave and saw the webby door. Behind it they could hear Moon-Face groaning and grumbling, and Saucepan humming one of his songs.

'Look—there's the end of the web, sticking out just there!' said Connie, pointing to the middle of the door.

'Who's there?' called Joe, from below.

'Me, Connie,' said Connie, 'and Beth too, and Jack and Jill, come to rescue you. We're going to undo the door.'

Jack pulled at the end of the web, and a thread unravelled. He wound it round and round the reel. Soon the door began to fall to pieces as all the thread was wound round the big cotton reel. Then the children could see inside the cave. They saw Moon-Face, Watzis-name, Saucepan, Joe and Frannie all in a heap together, bound tightly, but Joe called out to them in warning: 'Don't come near us or you'll be all messed up in this horrid sticky web.'

'I'm just going to find the end of the web that is binding you so tightly, and unravel it,' said Jack. 'Then you'll be free.'

He found the end of the thread, and soon he was unravelling it like wool, and the four prisoners rolled over and over on the floor as their bonds were pulled away. And at last they were free!

'Oooh! Thank you,' said Joe, sitting up. 'I feel better now that sticky stuff is off. What a lot you've got on that cotton reel, Jack!'

'Perhaps you would like to take it home and give it to Silky, as a little present,' said Jack. 'I know she often makes dresses, doesn't she?'

'Oh yes, she'd love it,' said Joe, taking it. 'Come on— let's get out of here and go home. I'm tired of Nursery Rhyme Land.'

'We promised the spider we'd block up the door of his cave so that you couldn't escape,' said Jack, with a grin. 'You get out first, and we'll put a stone here after!'

So they did. Then, taking the spider's big bath on his shoulder, Jack led the way back. 'Don't go near the window in case the spider sees you,' he said to Moon-Face and the others. 'I'll just bring little Miss Muffet out to say goodbye to you, then you can go.'

He went in with the bath. Miss Muffet had the kettle boiling and poured the water into it, adding some yellow mustard. She stirred it up and called to the spider:

'Come along—it's ready!'

He got out of the bed and put his feet into it, all eight of them. Then he suddenly looked up. 'I can hear my prisoners whispering together!' he said. 'They must have escaped. I must go after them!'

Back at Moon-Face's

Miss Muffet rushed to the door to warn the others to go. 'He's heard you whispering together!' she said. 'Go quickly!'

The children and the others all fled, Jack and Jill too. The spider took his feet out of the hot mustard bath and looked round for a towel to dry them.

'I won't give you a towel,' said Miss Muffet, severely. 'You can go after them with wet feet, and get an even worse cold, and be dreadfully ill. But I won't nurse you then.'

The spider sneezed. 'A wish-oo, a wish-oo! Oh dear, this is such a dreadful cold. I don't want to make it any worse. I'll be good and put my feet back. I'll have to let my prisoners escape.'

'There's a good spider,' said Miss Muffet.

He was pleased. 'I wish I could have a hot water bottle, Miss Muffet. I've never had one.'

'Well, as you've let your prisoners go, I'll lend you my hot water bottle,' said Miss Muffet, and went to get it.

Joe, Moon-Face, Saucepan and the others had by this time got to the top of the hill and down the other side. They looked back but could see no sign of the spider.

Back at Moon-Face's

'He's not coming after us, after all,' said Beth thankfully. 'Where's the hole through the cloud?'

'We'll show you,' said Jack and Jill. 'We'd like to come down it with you, and see the Faraway Tree.'

'Oh do!' said everyone. 'Come and have some dinner with us.'

'I'll send a message down to Silky and get her to come up and help to make some sandwiches,' said Moon-Face.

When they came to the hole in the cloud they all slid down the ladder and branch, and went to Moon-Face's house. Jack and Jill were amused to see his curved furniture.

They sent the red squirrel down to fetch Silky. She had been out shopping all morning, and came up delighted to know that Joe and the others were up the Tree. She was pleased to see Jack and Jill too.

'Hello!' she cried. 'It's ages since I saw you two. Do you still fall down the hill? Jack, you haven't got your head done up in vinegar and brown paper, for a change!'

'No—because Beth kindly helped me carry the pail of water down the hill today,' said Jack. 'And she goes faster than Jill, so we didn't fall over by getting out of step. We've had a lot of adventures today, Silky.'

'Oh, Silky, here's a present for you,' said Joe, remembering, and he gave the pretty little fairy the cotton reel with the spider thread wound onto it.

'Oh, thank you, Joe!' cried Silky. 'Just what I want! I couldn't get any fine thread at all this morning. This will do beautifully.'

73

The Folk of the Faraway Tree

'Will you help to make some sandwiches, Silky?' said Moon-Face. 'We thought we'd have a picnic dinner up here. Let me see—how many of us are there?'

'Six children—and four others,' counted Joe. 'Ten. You'll have to make about a hundred sandwiches!'

'It's a pity the Land of Goodies isn't here,' said Moon-Face. 'We could go up and take what food we wanted then and bring it down. Got any Google Buns or Pop-Cakes, Silky dear?'

'I've got some Pop-Cakes in my basket somewhere,' said Silky. 'Do Jack and Jill know them?'

They didn't, and they did enjoy them. They went pop as soon as they were put into the mouth, and honey flowed out from the middle of each cake!

'Delicious!' said Jack. 'I could do with a big box of these cakes.'

Soon they were all sitting on the broad branch outside Moon-Face's house, eating sandwiches and cakes and drinking lemonade.

There was as much lemonade as anyone wanted, because, in a friendly manner, the Faraway Tree suddenly began to grow ripe yellow lemons on the branches round about. All Moon-Face had to do was pick them, cut them in half, and squeeze them into a jug. Then he added water and sugar, and the children drank the lemonade!

'This is a marvellous tree,' said Connie, leaning back happily. 'Absolutely marvellous. You are clever, Moon-Face, to make such lovely lemonade.'

'Goodness me. Connie seems to be believing in the Tree at last,' said Joe. 'Do you, Connie?'

'Yes, I do,' said Connie. 'I can't help it. I didn't like that spider adventure—but this is lovely, sitting here and eating these delicious sandwiches and Pop-Cakes, and drinking lemonade from lemons growing on the Tree.'

She shook the branch she was leaning on, and some ripe lemons fell off. They went bumping down the Tree.

There came a yell from below.

'Now then! Who's throwing ripe lemons at me, I should like to know. One's got in my washtub. Any more of that and I'll come up and punish the thrower.'

'There!' said Moon-Face to Connie. 'See what you've done! Shaken down heaps of juicy lemons on to Dame Washalot. She'll be after you if you're not careful.'

'Oooh!' said Connie, in alarm. She called down the Tree. 'I'm sorry, Dame Washalot. It was an accident.'

'Connie's getting some manners,' said Joe to Beth. 'Any more Pop-Cakes? Have another, Saucepan?'

'Mother's very well, thank you,' said Saucepan.

'I said, "Have ANOTHER?"' said Joe.

'You haven't asked him to sell you a saucepan,' said Beth. 'Ask him about a saucepan to boil milk.'

'Oiled silk?' said Saucepan. 'No, my mother doesn't wear oiled silk. Why should she? She wears black, with a red shawl and a red bag and a bonnet with . . .'

'Can't we get away from Saucepan's mother?' groaned Joe. 'I never even knew he had one. I wonder where she lives.'

Saucepan unexpectedly heard this. 'She lives in the

Land of Dame Snap,' he said. 'She's works for her. She needs lots of saucepans because she has to cook meals for all the children at her school.'

'Gosh!' said Beth, remembering. 'We've been to Dame Snap's Land! We flew there once in a 'plane. We had an awful time because Dame Snap put us into her school!'

'Does your mother really live there?' said Joe. 'Do you ever go to see her?'

'Oh yes, when I can,' said Saucepan. 'I believe Dame Snap's land is coming next week. I'd like you all to meet my dear old mother. She will give you a wonderful dinner.'

There was a silence. No one wanted to be mixed up with Dame Snap again. She was a most unpleasant person.

'Well?' said Saucepan, looking round. 'I didn't hear anyone say "Thank you very much, we'd love to know your mother".'

'Well, you see—er—er—it's a bit awkward,' said Moon-Face. 'You see, your mother working for Dame Snap—er . . .'

'I suppose you are trying to say that my dear old mother isn't good enough for you to meet!' said Saucepan, unexpectedly, and looked terribly hurt and upset. 'All right. If you won't know my mother, you shan't know me!'

And to everyone's alarm he got up and walked straight up the branch into the cloud, and disappeared into the Land of Nursery Rhyme. Everyone yelled after him.

'Saucepan, we'd love to meet your mother, but we don't like Dame Snap!'

'Saucepan, come BACK!'

But Saucepan either didn't or wouldn't hear. 'You go and fetch him back,' said Joe to Jack and Jill. So up they went after him. But they soon came back.

'Can't see him anywhere,' they said. 'He isn't any-where to be found. I expect he is hiding himself away in a temper. He'll soon be back again.'

But Saucepan didn't come back.

'We'll have to go home,' said Joe, at last. 'Let us know when Saucepan comes back, Moon-Face. Tell him we would love to meet his old mother, and it's all a mistake. All the same—I hope he won't want us to go to Dame Snap's Land—I wouldn't like that at all.'

'Go down the slippery-slip,' said Moon-Face, throw-ing the children cushions. 'Yes, I feel upset about Saucepan too. He isn't usually so touchy. You go first, Joe.'

Joe sat on his cushion, gave himself a push and down he went, whizzing round and round the slippery-slip right to the bottom of the Tree.

He shot out of the trap door and landed on the tuft of moss. He got up hurriedly, knowing that Connie was coming down just behind him.

Soon all four were at the foot of the Tree. The squirrel collected the cushions and disappeared with them. Joe linked arms with the girls, and they turned towards home.

'Well, that was quite an adventure,' Joe said. 'I guess you don't want to meet Miss Muffet's spider again, Connie?'

'No, I don't,' said Connie. 'But I'd like to please old Saucepan, and meet his mother, even if he hasn't been very nice to me so far.'

'You're getting quite a nice little girl, Connie!' said Joe, in surprise. 'Well—maybe we'll all have to go and meet his mother next week. We'll see!'

Saucepan is Very Cross

For a few days the children did not hear anything from their friends in the Faraway Tree.

'I wonder if the Old Saucepan Man calmed down a bit and went back to Moon-Face's,' said Joe.

On the fifth or sixth day there came a knock at the door. Joe opened it. Outside was the red squirrel and he had a note in his paw.

'For you all,' he said, and gave it to Joe. 'I need an answer, please.'

Joe slit the envelope and read the note out loud.

'DEAR EVERYBODY,

'When are you coming to see us again? Old Saucepan came back yesterday from the Land of Nursery Rhyme. He had been staying with Polly-Put-The-Kettle-On. He gave her a new kettle, and she said he could stay with her in return. He is still upset because he says we don't want to meet his dear old mother. He won't speak to any of us. He is living with the Owl, and he has made up a lot of rude songs about us. Will you come and see if you can put things right? He might listen to you. He won't take any notice of me or

Silky or Watzisname. So do come.

> 'Love from
> 'MOON-FACE'.

'Well!' said Joe, putting the note back into its envelope. 'Funny old Saucepan! Who would have thought he would be so touchy? Why, I'd love to meet his mother. She must be a dear old thing.'

'It's only that she works in Dame Snap's school and if we go and see her, Dame Snap might catch us again,' said Beth. 'We had an awful time with her last time.'

'We'd better go up the Tree tomorrow, and tell Saucepan exactly what we think, and make sure he hears and understands us,' said Frannie. 'Let's do that.'

'Is that the answer then?' asked the red squirrel, politely.

'Yes, that's the answer,' said Joe. 'We'll be up the Tree tomorrow—and we'll try and put things right. Tell Moon-Face that.'

The squirrel bounded off. The children watched him. 'What a dependable little fellow that squirrel is,' said Joe. 'Well—we must go up the Tree tomorrow, no doubt about that. Coming, Connie?'

'Oh yes,' said Connie, beginning to feel excited again. 'Of course. I'd love to, Joe.'

So the next day, the four children went off to the Faraway Tree. 'We'll climb up,' said Joe. 'Because if Saucepan is living in the Owl's home, it's only just a little way past the Angry Pixie's, and we can call for him there.'

So, when they came to the Tree, they didn't send for cushions to go up on, but began to climb. The Tree was growing blackberries, ripe and juicy. It was fun to pick them, and bite into them, feeling the rich, sweet juice squirt out.

All of them had blackberry stained mouths as they climbed. They came to the Angry Pixie's and Connie kept well away from the window this time. But his door was open, and he was out. A small field-mouse was busy scrubbing the floor, and another one was shaking the mats.

'Bit of spring cleaning going on,' said Joe, as they passed. 'I suppose the Angry Pixie's gone out for the day, to get away from it!'

Soon they came to the Owl's home. They peeped cautiously in at the window. Saucepan was there, polishing his kettles at top speed, making them shine brightly. He was singing one of his silly songs, very loudly:

> 'Two scoldings for Connie,
> Two shakings for Joe,
> Two snarlings for Beth,
> Hi-Tiddley-ho!'

> 'Two drubbings for Moon-Face,
> Two snubbings for Fran,
> Two snappings for Silky,
> From the old Saucepan Man!'

'Gosh! He must still be in a very bad temper,' said Beth, quite hurt. 'And imagine talking about snapping at Silky. He's always been so fond of her.'

81

'Do you think we'd better stop and talk to him now or not?' said Joe.

'Not,' said Frannie at once. 'He'll only be rude and horrid. Let's go up to Moon-Face and Silky, and see what they suggest.'

So up the Tree they went, leaving behind the cross old Saucepan Man, still polishing his kettles. They just dodged Dame Washalot's water in time. They heard it coming and darted to the other side of the Tree. They waited till it had all gone down, then climbed up again.

They came to Silky's house and knocked at the door. Moon-Face opened it, and smiled.

'Hello! So you've come all right! Come in. I was just having a cup of hot chocolate with Silky.'

They all crowded into Silky's dear little tree house and sat down. Silky poured them out cups of hot chocolate, and handed round some new Pop-Cakes. How Connie loved the pop they made, and the honey that flowed out from the middle! She sat enjoying her lunch and listened to the others talking.

'Saucepan is really awful,' said Silky. 'He sings rude songs about us all day long, and all the Tree folk laugh!'

'Yes, We heard the songs,' said Joe. 'Not very kind of him, is it? What can we do about it? Will he listen to us, do you think, if we go back and talk nicely to him?'

'I don't know,' said Moon-Face, doubtfully. 'When Silky and I went down to fetch him last night to beg him to be sensible and to be friends, he sang his songs at us, and did his clashing, clanging dance. He frightened everyone in the Tree, and Dame Washalot sent a message to say that if the noise went on she would empty twenty washtubs down at once, and drown us all!'

'We can't let Saucepan go on like this,' said Beth. 'How can we make him feel better, and ashamed of his rude behaviour?'

'I know!' said Connie, unexpectedly. 'Let's go down and take presents for his mother. Then he will be so pleased he will be nice again.'

Everyone stared at Connie. 'Well, isn't that a splendid idea!' said Silky. 'Why didn't we think of it before? Saucepan will be thrilled!'

'Yes, really, Connie, that's a great idea!' said Beth, and Connie went red with pleasure. The others ticked her off so much that it was very pleasant to be praised for a change.

'Connie's getting quite nice,' Frannie said to Silky and Moon-Face. 'Now she has to live with us, she's different—not so silly and selfish. You'll get to like her soon.'

'It's a good idea, to take presents to Saucepan for his mother,' said Moon-Face. 'We'll do that. It's the one thing that will make him smile. What shall we take?'

'I'll look in my treasure bag,' said Silky, 'and you go up to your house and see if you've got anything that would please an old lady, Moon-Face.'

Moon-Face went off. The others watched as Silky turned out what she called her 'treasure bag.' It had lots of pretty things in it.

'Here's a lovely set of buttons,' said Silky, picking up a set of red buttons, made like poppies. 'She'd like those.'

83

'And what about this pink rose for a bonnet?' said Beth, picking up a rose that looked so real she was sure it must have a smell. It had! 'This would do beautifully for an old lady.'

'And here's a hat pin with a little rabbit sitting at one end,' said Frannie. 'She'd like that.'

Just then Moon-Face came back. He brought with him three things—a tiny vase for flowers, a brooch with 'M' on it for Mother, and a shoe-horn made of silver. The others thought they would be lovely for the old lady.

'We can take one thing each and give it to Saucepan for his mother,' said Moon-Face. 'Come on! We'll let Silky do the talking. Saucepan likes her best. Don't let him see you at first, Connie. He doesn't like you very much.'

They all went down to the Owl's home. They peeped inside. Saucepan had finished polishing his kettles, and was sitting silently, looking gloomy.

'Go on, Silky!' whispered Moon-Face. So Silky went in first, holding out the pink rose.

'Dear Saucepan, I've brought you a present to give to your mother from me, when you see her,' she said, in her very loudest voice. Incredibly, Saucepan heard every word. He looked at Silky, and said nothing at first. Then he said:

'For my old mother? Oh, how kind of you, Silky! She'll love this pink rose.'

'Quick, come on!' whispered Moon-Face to the others. So they all crowded in, holding out their gifts nervously, and saying, 'For your mother, Saucepan.'

Saucepan put each gift solemnly into one of his kettles or saucepans. He seemed very touched.

'Thank you,' he said. 'Thank you very much. My mother will be delighted. It's her birthday soon. I will take her these presents from you. I expect she will invite you to her birthday party.'

'That would be very nice,' said Joe, in a loud voice. 'But Saucepan, we don't like Dame Snap, and you said your mother worked for her. If we go to see her, will you promise we don't get put into Dame Snap's school again? We went there once and she was horrid to us.'

'Oh, of course I'll see to that,' said the old Saucepan Man, who looked quite his old cheery self again. 'I'm sorry I sang rude songs about you. It was all a mistake. I'll go up into Dame Snap's Land tomorrow and see my dear old mother, and take your gifts and messages. Then you can come and join us for her birthday party.'

'All right!' said Joe. 'We'd like to do that—but mind, Saucepan, we don't want to see Dame Snap even in the distance.'

'You won't,' said Saucepan.

But oh dear—they did!

In the Land of Dame Snap

It wasn't very long before a message came from Moon-Face. 'I have heard from Saucepan. He says we must go up to Dame Snap's land tomorrow, and meet his mother. If we go to the back door of the school, she will be there.'

So the next day, the four children set off. They went up the Faraway Tree, and called for Silky first. She was wearing a pretty party dress, and had washed her hair, which looked more like a golden mist than ever.

'I'm just ready,' she said, giving her hair a last brush. 'I hope Moon-Face won't keep us waiting. He lost his hat this morning, and he's been rushing up and down the Tree all day, asking everyone if they've seen it.'

When they got to Moon-Face's he was quite ready, beaming as usual, a floppy hat on his head.

'Oh, you found your hat then?' said Silky.

'Yes—it had fallen down the slippery-slip,' said Moon-Face. 'And when I went down there, I shot out of the trap door at the bottom, and there was my hat on my feet! So that was all right. Are we all ready?'

'Yes,' said Joe. 'But for goodness' sake do look out for Dame Snap. I feel very nervous of her.'

'Saucepan will be looking out for us, don't worry,' said Moon-Face. 'I expect he will be at the top of the ladder, waiting. We're sure to have a lovely meal. His mother is a wonderful cook.'

They climbed up the topmost branch of the Tree, and came to the ladder. They all went up it and found themselves in Dame Snap's Land. There wasn't much to see—only, in the distance, a large green house set in the middle of a great garden.

'That's Dame Snap's School,' said Joe to Connie.

'Who goes to it?' asked Connie, curiously.

'All the bad pixies and fairies and elves,' said Beth. 'We saw some once when we were there. Dame Snap has to be very strict or she wouldn't be able to teach them. They are very naughty.'

'Where's the back door?' said Connie, looking nervously around. 'Let's go there, quick. I do wish Saucepan had waited for us at the top of the ladder.'

'Yes, I don't know why he didn't,' said Moon-Face, puzzled. 'Shall we call him?'

'No, of course not, silly!' said Joe. 'We'll have Dame Snap after us at once! Come on—we'll find the back door. We really can't wait about any longer.'

So they went round the large garden, keeping carefully outside the high wall, until they came to two gates. One opened on to the drive that led to the front door. The other opened on to a path that clearly led to the back door.

'This is where we go,' said Beth, and they went quietly through the back gate. They came to the back door. It was shut. No one seemed to be about.

'I suppose Saucepan and his mother are expecting us?' said Joe, puzzled. He knocked on the door. There was no answer. He knocked again.

'Let's open the door and go in,' said Beth, impatiently. 'We must find Saucepan. I expect he's forgotten he asked us to come today.'

They pushed the door open and went into a big and very tidy kitchen. There was no one there. It was very strange. Connie opened another door and peered into what seemed to be a big hall.

'I think I can hear someone,' she said. 'I'll go and see if it's Saucepan.'

Before the others could stop her she had opened the door and gone. No one felt like following. They sat down in the kitchen and waited.

Connie went into the big hall. There was no one there. She went into another room, that looked like a living room. Connie peered round it in curiosity. Then, through a door opposite came a tall, old woman, with large spectacles on her long nose and a big white bonnet on her head.

'Oh!' said Connie, beaming. 'Happy birthday! Where's Saucepan? We've all come to meet you!'

The old woman stopped in surprise. 'Indeed!' she said. 'You have, have you? And who are the rest of you?'

'Oh—didn't Saucepan tell you?' asked Connie. 'There's Joe and Beth and Frannie and Moon-Face and Silky. We did hope that Saucepan would meet us by the ladder, because we were so afraid of meeting that awful Dame Snap.'

'Oh, really?' said the old woman, and her eyes gleamed behind her big spectacles. 'You think she's awful, do you?'

'Well, Joe and the others told me all about her,' said Connie. 'They were all here once, you know, and they escaped. They were very afraid of meeting her again.'

'Where are they?' said the old woman.

'In the kitchen,' said Connie. 'I'll go and tell them I've found you.'

She ran ahead of the old woman, who followed her at once. Connie flung open the kitchen door.

'I've found Saucepan's mother!' she said. 'Here she is!'

The old lady came into the kitchen—and Joe and the others gave a gasp of horror. It wasn't Saucepan's mother. It was Dame Snap herself, looking absolutely furious.

'Dame Snap!' yelled Joe. 'Run, everyone!'

But it was too late. Dame Snap turned the key in the kitchen door and put it into her pocket.

'So you escaped from me before, did you?' she said. 'Well, you won't escape again. Bad children who are sent to me to be good don't usually escape before they are taught things they ought to know!'

'Look here!' began Moon-Face, putting a bold face on. 'Look here, Dame Snap, we didn't come to see you; we came to see Saucepan's mother.'

'I've never in my life heard of Saucepan,' said Dame Snap. 'Never. It's a naughty story. You're making it up. I punish people for telling stories. You wicked man!' she snapped at Moon-Face.

'Saucepan's mother works for you!' he shouted, dodging round the kitchen. 'She cooks for your school! Where is she?'

'Oh—the lady who cooks,' said Dame Snap. 'Well, she walked out yesterday, along with a dreadful creature who had kettles and pans hung all round him.'

'That was Saucepan,' groaned Joe. 'Where did they go?'

'I don't know and I certainly don't care,' said Dame Snap. 'The lady was rude to me, and I shouted at her. So she went off. Can any of you cook?'

'I can,' said Beth. 'But if you think I'm going to cook for you, you're mistaken. I'm going home.'

'You can stay here and cook meals for the school till I get someone else,' said Dame Snap. 'And this girl can help you.' She pointed to Frannie. 'The others can come into my school and learn to work hard, to get good manners and to be well behaved. Go along now!'

To Joe's horror, she pushed everyone but Beth and Frannie into the hall, and up the stairs to a big classroom, where lots of noisy little elves, fairies and pixies were playing and pushing and fighting together.

Dame Snap dealt a few scoldings and sent them to their seats, yelling.

Connie was very afraid. She stayed close to Joe and Moon-Face. Dame Snap made them all sit down at the back of the room.

'Silence!' she snapped. 'You will now do your homework. The new pupils will please find pencils and paper in their desks. Everyone must answer the questions on the blackboard. If anyone gets them wrong, they will have to be punished.'

'Oh dear!' groaned Silky. Connie whispered to her:

'Don't worry! I'm very good at lessons. I will know

all the answers, and I'll tell you them too.'

'Who is whispering?' shouted Dame Snap, and everyone jumped. 'You, new girl, come out here.'

Connie came out, trembling. Dame Snap gave her a sharp scolding.

'Stop crying!' she snapped. And Connie stopped. She gave a gulp, and stopped at once.

'Go back to your seat and do your homework,' ordered the old Dame. So back Connie went.

'Now, no talking and no playing,' said Dame Snap. 'Just hard work. I am going to talk to my new kitchen staff about a nice syrup pudding. If I hear anyone talking or playing when I come back, or if anyone hasn't done the homework, there will be no nice syrup pudding for any of you.'

With this threat Dame Snap walked out of the room. She left the door wide open so that she could hear any noise.

The pixie in front of Connie turned round and shook his pen on her book. A big blot came out! The goblin next to him pulled Silky's hair. A bright-eyed pixie threw a pencil at Moon-Face and hit him on the nose. Dame Snap's pupils were a really naughty lot!

'We must do our homework!' whispered Silky to the others. 'Connie, read the questions on the blackboard, and tell us the answers, quick!'

So Connie read them—but, oh dear, how could she answer questions like that? She never could. They would all go without syrup pudding, and be scolded and sent to bed! Oh dear, oh dear!

Dame Snap's School

The more the children looked at the three questions on the blackboard, the more they felt certain they could never answer them. Moon-Face turned to Connie. 'Quick! Tell us the right answers. You said you were good at lessons.'

Connie read the first question. 'Three blackbirds sat on a cherry tree. They ate one hundred and twenty three of the cherries. How many were left?'

'Well, how can we say, unless we know how many there were in the beginning?' said Connie, out loud. 'What a silly question!'

Joe read the next one out loud. 'If there are a hundred pages in a book, how many books would there be on the shelf?'

'The questions are just nonsense,' said Moon-Face, gloomily.

'They were before, when we were here,' said Joe.

The third question was very short. Joe read it out. 'Why is a blackboard?'

'Why is a blackboard!' repeated Silky. 'There is no sense in that question either.'

'Well—the questions are nonsense, so we'll put down answers that are nonsense,' said Joe.

So they put down 'none' about how many cherries were left on the tree. Then they read the book question again. And again they put down 'none'.

'We are not told that the shelf was a book shelf,' said Joe. 'It might be a shelf for ornaments, or a bathroom shelf for glasses and tooth brushes and things. There wouldn't be any books there.'

The third question was really puzzling. 'Why is a blackboard?'

Joe ran out of his place and rubbed out the two last words. He wrote them again—and then the question read 'Why is a board black?'

'We can easily answer that,' said Joe, with a grin. 'Why is a board black? So that we can write on it with white chalk!'

So, when Dame Snap came back, the only people who had answered all the questions were Joe, Silky, Moon-Face and Connie! Dame Snap smiled at them.

'Dear me, I have some clever children at last!' she said. 'You have written answers to all the questions.'

'Are they right then?' asked Silky, in surprise.

'I don't know,' said Dame Snap. 'But that doesn't matter. It's the answers I want. I don't care what's in them, so long as you have written answers. I don't know the answers myself, so it's no good me reading them.'

Then Moon-Face undid all the good they had done by giving an extremely rude snort. 'Pooh! What a silly school this is! Fancy giving people questions if you don't know the answers! Pooh!'

'Don't "pooh" at me like that!' said Dame Snap,

getting angry all of a sudden. Go to bed! Off to bed with you for the rest of the day!'

'But—but,' began poor Moon-Face, in alarm, wishing he had not spoken, 'but . . .'

'You'll turn into a goat in a minute, if you are so full of "buts," said Dame Snap, and she pushed Moon-Face out of the door. She drove the others out too, and took them to a small bedroom, with four tiny beds, very hard and narrow.

'Now, into bed you get, and nothing but bread and water for you all day long. I will not have rudeness in my school!'

She shut the door and locked it. Moon-Face looked at the others in dismay. 'I'm sorry I made her do this,' he said. 'Very sorry. But really, she did make me feel so angry. Do you think we'd better go to bed? She might punish us if we don't.'

Connie leapt into bed at once, fully dressed. She wasn't going to risk Dame Snap coming back and punishing her! The others did the same. They drew the quilts up to their chins and lay there gloomily. This was a horrid adventure—just when they had looked forward so much to coming out to the birthday party.

'I wonder what Beth and Frannie are doing,' said Moon-Face. 'Hard work, I suppose. I do think Saucepan might have warned us that his mother had gone. It's too bad.'

Just then there came the sound of a song floating up from outside.

Dame Snap's School

'Two worms for a sparrow,
Two slugs for a duck,
Two snails for a blackbird,
Two hens for a cluck!'

'Saucepan! It must be Saucepan!' cried everyone, and jumped out of bed and ran to the window. Outside, far below, stood Saucepan, and with him were Beth and Frannie, giggling.

'Hi, Saucepan! Here we are!' cried Joe. 'We're locked in.'

Dame Snap smiled at them.

'Oh—we wondered where you were,' said Saucepan, grinning. 'Dame Snap's locked in, too—locked into the store room by young Beth here. She was just doing it when I came along to see if you had arrived.'

'Arrived! We've been here ages,' said Joe, indignantly. 'Why didn't you come to warn us?'

'My watch must be wrong again,' said Saucepan. He usually kept it in one of his kettles, but as it shook about there every day, it wasn't a very good time keeper. 'Never mind. I'll rescue you now.'

A terrific banging noise came from somewhere downstairs. 'That's Dame Snap in the store room,' said Saucepan. 'She's in a dreadful temper.'

'Well, for goodness' sake, help us out of here,' said Connie, alarmed. 'How can we get out? The door's locked, and I heard Dame Snap taking the key out the other side.'

Crash! Bang! Clatter!

'Sounds as if Dame Snap is throwing a few pies and things about,' said Joe. 'Saucepan, how can we get out of here?'

'I'll just undo the rope that hangs my things round me,' said Saucepan, and he began to untie the rope round his waist. He undid it, and then, to the children's surprise, his kettles and saucepans began to peel off him. They were each tied firmly to the rope.

'Saucepan does look funny without his kettles and pans round him,' said Connie in surprise. 'I hardly know him!'

Saucepan took the end of the rope and tied a stone to it. He threw it up to the window. Joe caught the stone and pulled on the rope. It came up, laden here and there with kettles and saucepans.

'Tie the rope end to a bed,' called Saucepan. 'Then come down the rope. You can use the kettles and saucepans as steps. They are tied on tightly.'

So, very cautiously, Moon-Face, Joe, Silky and a very nervous Connie climbed down the rope, using the saucepans and kettles as steps. They were very glad to stand on firm ground again!

'Well, there we are,' said Saucepan, pleased. 'Wasn't that a good idea?'

'Yes—but how are we to get your kettles and saucepans back for you?' said Joe.

'It doesn't matter at all,' said Saucepan. 'I can take as many as I can carry out of the kitchen here. They are what I gave my mother each birthday, you know, so they are hers.'

He went into the kitchen and collected a great selection of kettles and saucepans. He tied them all to the rope used for a washing line, and then once more became the Old Saucepan Man they knew so well, with pans of all shapes and sizes hung all round him!

Crash! Smash! Clang! Dame Snap was getting angrier and angrier in the store room. She kicked and she stamped.

'Dame Snap!' cried Joe, suddenly, and he stood outside the locked store room door. 'I will ask you a question, and if you can tell me the answer, I will set you free. Now, be quiet and listen.'

There was a silence in the store room. Joe asked his question.

'If Saucepan takes twelve kettles from your kitchen, how long does it take to boil a cup of hot chocolate on a Friday?'

The others giggled. There came an angry cry from the store room. 'It's a silly question, and there's no answer. Let me out at once!'

'It's the same kind of question you asked us!' said Joe. 'I'm sorry you can't answer it. I can't either. So you must stay where you are, till one of your school children is kind enough to let you out. Goodbye, dear Dame Snap!'

The children and the others went out giggling into the garden. 'Where are we going now?' asked Beth. 'Where's your mother, Saucepan?'

'She's in the Land of Tea Parties,' said Saucepan. 'It's not very far. I took her there because it's her birthday, you know, and I thought she'd like to have a party without going to any trouble. Shall we go?'

So, hearing Dame Snap's furious cries and bangs gradually fading behind them, the little group set off together, very glad to have escaped from Dame Snap in safety.

'Come on—here's the boundary between this land and the next. Jump!' said Saucepan.

They jumped—and over they went into the Land of Tea Parties! What a fine time they meant to have there!

The Land of Tea Parties

The Land of Tea Parties was peculiar. It seemed to be made up of nothing but white-covered tables laden with all kinds of good things to eat!

'Gosh!' said Joe, looking round. 'What a lot of tables—big and small, round and square—and all filled with the most gorgeous things to eat!'

'They've got chairs set round them too,' said Frannie. 'All ready for people to sit on.'

'And look at the little waiters!' said Connie, in delight. 'They are rabbits!'

So they were—rabbits dressed neatly in aprons, and little black coats, hurrying here and there, carrying jugs of lemonade and all kinds of other drinks.

It was lovely to watch them; they were so very busy and so very serious.

'There are some people choosing tables already!' said Joe, pointing. 'Look—that must be a pixie's birthday party, sitting over there. Aren't they sweet?'

'And oh, look!—there's a squirrel's party,' said Frannie. 'Mother and Father Squirrel, and all the baby squirrels. I expect it's one of the baby squirrels' birthdays!'

It was fun to see the little parties. But soon the children began to feel very hungry. There were such nice things on the tables! There were sandwiches of all kinds, with little labels showing what they were. Frannie read some of them out loud.

'Dewdrop and honey sandwiches—ooh! And here are some tunafish and strawberry sandwiches—what a funny mixture! But I dare say it would be nice. And here are oranges and lemon sandwiches—I've never heard of those. And pineapple and cucumber! Really, what an exciting lot of things!'

'Look at the cakes!' said Connie. 'I've never seen such beauties.'

Nor had anyone else. There were pink cakes, yellow cakes, chocolate cakes, ginger cakes, cakes with fruit and silver balls all over them, cakes with frosting, cakes with flowers made from sugar, cakes as big as could be, and tiny ones only enough for two people.

There were desserts and fruit salads and ice creams too. Which table should they choose? There were different things at every table!

'Here's one with chocolate ice cream,' said Connie. 'Let's have this one.'

'No—I'd like this one—it's got blue cakes, and I've never seen those before,' said Silky.

'Well, shouldn't we find Saucepan's mother before we do anything?' said Moon-Face.

'Gosh, of course we should!' said Beth. 'Seeing all those gorgeous things made me forget we had come to celebrate Saucepan's mother's birthday. SAUCEPAN, WHERE IS YOUR MOTHER?'

'Over there,' said Saucepan, and he pointed to where the dearest little old woman stood waiting, her apple cheeks rosy red, and her bright eyes twinkling as brightly as Saucepan's. 'She's waiting. She's got the pink rose in her bonnet, look!—and the hat pin—and she's sewn the red poppy buttons on her dress, and she's pinned the M for Mother brooch in front. The only thing she can't wear are the shoe horn and the vase, and I think she's got them in her pocket. She was really pleased with everything.'

'Let's go and wish her a happy birthday,' said Beth, so they all went over to the little old lady, and wished her a very happy birthday. She was delighted to see them all, and she kissed them, each one, even Moon-Face.

'Well, I am glad you've come,' she said. 'I began to think something had happened to you.'

'It had,' said Joe, and he began to tell her about Dame Snap. But old Mrs Saucepan was just as deaf as Saucepan was himself.

'Here you are at last,' said Mrs Saucepan to Saucepan.

'Yes, we did come fast,' agreed Saucepan. 'We locked up Dame Snap.'

'Locked up the cat?' said Mrs Saucepan. 'Why?'

The children giggled. Joe went up to Mrs Saucepan and spoke very clearly.

'Let's have some food! The tables are getting filled up!'

Mrs Saucepan heard. 'Yes, we will,' she said.

'I'd like the table with blue cakes,' said Silky.

'I'd like the one with pineapple and cucumber sandwiches,' said Connie.

'Well—as it's Saucepan's mother's birthday, don't

you think we should let her choose the table?' said Beth. 'She should have the things she likes best today.'

'Yes, of course,' said the others, rather ashamed not to have thought of that. 'MRS SAUCEPAN, PLEASE CHOOSE YOUR OWN TABLE.'

Well, Mrs Saucepan went straight to the big round table, set with eight chairs, and sat down at the head of it—and wasn't it strange, there were blue cakes there for Silky, pineapple and cucumber sandwiches for Connie, a big fat chocolate cake for Moon-Face, and all the things the others wanted too!

'This is fantastic,' said Connie, beginning on the sandwiches. 'Oh—I never tasted such beautiful sand-wiches in my life, never!'

The little rabbit waiters ran up, and smiled at old Mrs Saucepan. 'What will you have to drink?' they asked.

'Hot chocolate for me,' said Mrs Saucepan. 'What for you others?'

'Lemonade! Soda! Orange juice!' called the children and the others. The rabbits ran off, and came back with bottles of everything asked for, and a big jug of hot chocolate for Mrs Saucepan.

What fun they all had! There were squeals of laugh-ter from everyone, and from every table there came happy chattering. The Land of Tea Parties was a great success.

The children finished up with ice cream. Then the rabbits brought round big boxes of presents and they shared them all out. There were brooches, and rings, and little toys, and everyone had a funny paper hat to wear.

'Well, we've had a fabulous time,' said Joe, at last,

'but I think we should go now, Mrs Saucepan. Thank you very much for asking us here. I hope you get another job somewhere soon.'

'Oh, I think I shall go and live in the Faraway Tree with Dame Washalot,' said Mrs Saucepan. 'She's always so busy with her washing, she hasn't much time to do anything else. I could do the cooking for her. I could make cakes to sell too, and have a little shop there.'

'Oh—that would be lovely!' cried Beth. 'I'll often come and buy some from you.'

'We'd better go back through the Land of Dame Snap very cautiously indeed,' said Moon-Face. 'We can't get back to the Tree from this land because it's not over the Tree. We'll have to creep back through Dame Snap's Land and rush to the ladder quickly.'

So they said goodbye to the busy little rabbit waiters, and jumped over the boundary line again, back into Dame Snap's Land. They had to pass near the school, of course, and they listened carefully to find out what was going on.

There was a terrific commotion of shouting, laughing and squealing. The grounds of the school were full of the school children, and what a time they were having!

'Old Dame Snap must still be in the store room,' said Moon-Face. 'Yes, listen—I believe I can still hear her hammering away!'

Sure enough, over all the noise made by the school children, there came the sound of hammering!

'Shouldn't we set her free?' said Frannie, rather

alarmed. 'She might stay there for ages and starve to death!'

'Don't be silly! How can she starve when she is surrounded by food of all kinds?' said Moon-Face. 'It will be the children who will go hungry! I guess when they are hungry enough they will open the door and let Dame Snap out all right! Gosh, what a bad temper she will be in.'

They all hurried through the land at top speed, half afraid that Dame Snap might be let out before they were safe, and come after them. Still, they had Mrs Saucepan with them, and if anyone had to stand up to Dame Snap, she certainly would.

At last they came to the ladder sticking up into the land from the cloud below.

'You go first, Moon-Face, and help Mrs Saucepan down,' said Joe. So down went Moon-Face, and politely and carefully helped the old lady down the little yellow ladder, through the cloud and on to the topmost branch of the Tree.

Everyone followed, breathing sighs of relief to be safely away from Dame Snap once more. Nobody ever wanted to visit her land again!

'We really must say goodbye now,' said Joe to the Tree folk. 'Shall we just take Mrs Saucepan down to Dame Washalot for you, Saucepan?'

'I'll come too,' said Saucepan, hearing what was said. So down they went, and when Dame Washalot saw old Mrs Saucepan, she was very excited. She threw her soapy arms round the old lady's neck and hugged her.

'I hope you've come to stay!' she said. 'I've always

wanted you to live in the Faraway Tree.'

'Goodbye, Mrs Saucepan,' said Beth. 'I shall come and buy your cakes the very first day you put them on sale. I do hope you've had a happy birthday.'

'The nicest one I've ever had!' said the old lady, smiling. 'Goodbye my dears, and hurry home!'

In the Land of Secrets

Connie could not forget the exciting Faraway Tree, and the different lands that came at the top. She asked the others about all the different lands they had been to, and begged and begged them to take her to the next one.

'We'll see what Moon-Face says,' said Joe at last. 'We don't go to every land, Connie. You wouldn't like to go to the Land of Whizz-About, for instance, would you? Moon-Face once went there, and he said he couldn't bear it—everything went at such a pace, and he was out of breath the whole time.'

'Well, I think it sounds rather exciting,' said Connie, who was intensely curious about everything to do with the different lands. 'Oh, Joe, let's find out what land is there next. I really must go.'

'All right,' said Joe. 'We'll ask Mother if we can have a day out tomorrow, and we'll go up the Tree if you like. But mind—if there is a horrid land, we're not going. We've had too many narrow escapes now, to risk getting caught somewhere nasty.'

Mother said they could go up the Tree the next day. 'I'll give you sandwiches, if you like, and you can have lunch in the Wood or up the Tree, whichever you like,' she told them.

'Oh, up the Tree!' cried Connie. So, when the next day came, she wore old clothes without even being told! She was learning to be sensible at last.

They set off soon after breakfast. They hadn't let Silky or Moon-Face know they were coming, but they felt sure they would be in the Tree.

They jumped over the ditch and made their way through the whispering Wood till they came to the Faraway Tree. Joe whistled for the red squirrel to tell him to go up and ask Moon-Face to send cushions down. But the red squirrel didn't come.

'Bother!' said Beth. 'Now we'll have to climb up, and it's so hot!'

So up they climbed. The Angry Pixie was sitting at his window, which was wide open. He waved to them, and Connie was glad to see he had no ink or water to throw at her.

'Going up to the Land of Secrets?' he shouted to them.

'Oh—is the Land of Secrets there?' cried Joe. 'It sounds exciting. What's it like?'

'Oh—just secrets!' said the Angry Pixie. 'You can usually find out anything you badly want to know. I believe Watzisname wanted to try and find out exactly what his real name is, so maybe he'll visit it too.'

'I'd like to know some secrets too,' said Connie.

'What secrets do you want to know?' asked Joe.

'Oh—I'd like to know how much money the old man who lives next door to us at home has got,' said Connie. 'And I'd like to know what Mrs Toms at home has done to make people not speak to her—and . . .'

107

'What an awful girl you are!' said Beth. 'Those are other people's secrets, not yours. Fancy wanting to find out other people's secrets!'

'Yes, it's not nice of you, Connie,' said Frannie. 'Joe, don't let Connie go into the Land of Secrets if that's the kind of thing she wants to find out. She's gone all curious and prying again, like she used to be.'

Connie was angry. She went red and glared at the others. 'Well, don't you want to know secrets too?' she said. 'You said you did!'

'Yes, but not other people's,' said Joe at once. 'I'd like to know where to find the very first violets for instance, so that I could surprise Mother on her birthday with a great big bunch. They are her favourite flowers.'

'And I'd like to know the secret of curly hair, so that I could use it on all my dolls,' said Beth.

'And I'd like to know the secret of growing lettuces with big hearts,' said Frannie. 'Mine never grow nice ones.'

'What silly secrets!' said Connie.

'Better to want to know a silly secret than a horrid one, or one that doesn't belong to you,' said Joe. 'All you want to do is to poke your nose into other people's affairs, Connie, and that's a horrid thing to do.'

Connie climbed the Tree, not speaking a word to the others. She was very angry with them. She was so angry that she didn't look out for Dame Washalot's water coming down the Tree, and it suddenly swished all round her and soaked her.

That made her angrier still, especially when the others laughed at her. 'All right!' said Connie, in a nasty voice. 'I'll find out your secrets too—where you've put your new book so that I can't borrow it, Joe—and where you've put your paints, Beth—and I'll find out which of your dolls you like the best, Frannie, and hide her!'

'You really are a nasty child,' said Joe. 'You won't go up into the Land of Secrets, so don't worry yourself about all these things!'

They climbed up to Silky's house, but the door was shut. They went up to Moon-Face's, but his door was shut too. The Old Saucepan Man was not about and neither was Watzisname. Nobody seemed to be about at all.

'Perhaps Saucepan's mother would know,' said Beth. So they climbed down to Dame Washalot, and found old Mrs Saucepan there.

'Saucepan and Watzisname have both gone up into the Land of Secrets,' she told them, 'but I don't know about Silky and Moon-Face—I expect they have gone with them, though Saucepan didn't tell me they were going. Have a cake?'

Old Mrs Saucepan was already busy making all kinds of delicious cakes and pies, ready to open her shop on Dame Washalot's broad branch. Two goblins were busy making a stall for her. She meant to open her little shop the next day.

The children took their cakes with thanks. They were really delicious.

They climbed up the Tree again to Moon-Face's house. Joe turned the handle. The door opened, but the curved room inside was empty.

'What a nuisance!' said Joe. 'Now what shall we do?'

'We might as well go up into the Land of Secrets, and find the others, and have our picnic with them,' said Frannie.

'Yes,' said Connie, who was dying to go up into this new land.

'Well, but we didn't want Connie to go,' said Joe. 'She'll only go prying into other people's secrets, and we can't have that.'

'I won't try and find out your secrets,' said Connie. 'I promise I won't.'

'I don't know if I trust you,' said Joe. 'But still, we can't go without you. So, if you do come, Connie, just be careful—and remember that you might get into trouble if you're not careful.'

'I wonder if old Watzisname has found out what his real name is,' said Beth, beginning to climb up the topmost branch. 'I'd love to know it. It would be nice to call him something else. Watzisname is a silly name.'

They all went up the topmost branch, and up the yellow ladder through the hole in the cloud, and then into the Land of Secrets.

It was a curious land, quiet, perfectly still, and a sort of twilight hung over it. There was no sun to be seen at all.

'It feels secret and solemn!' said Joe, with a little shiver. 'I'm not sure if I like it.'

'Come on!' said Beth. 'Let's go and find the others and see how we get to know secrets.'

They came to a hill, with several coloured doors in it, set with sparkling stones that glittered in the curious twilight.

'They must be the doors of caves,' said Joe. 'Look!—there are names on the doors.'

The children read them. They were peculiar names. 'Witch Know-a-Lot.' 'The Enchanter Wise-Man.' 'Dame Tell-You-All.' 'Mrs Hidden.' 'The Wizard Tall-Hat.'

'They all sound really clever and wise and informed,' said Joe. 'Hello! Here's somebody coming.'

A tall fairy was coming along, carrying a pair of wings. She stopped and spoke to the children.

'Do you know where Dame Tell-You-All lives, please? I want to know how to fasten on these wings and fly with them.'

'She lives in that cave,' said Beth, pointing to where a door had 'Dame Tell-You-All' painted on it in big letters.

'Thank you,' said the fairy, and rapped sharply on the door. It opened and she went inside. It shut. In about half a minute it opened again, and out came the fairy, this time with the wings on her back. She rose into the air and flew off, waving to the children.

'The Dame's really clever!' she cried. 'I can fly now. Look!'

'This is an exciting place,' said Beth. 'Goodness, the things we could learn! I wish I had a pair of wings. I've a good mind to go and ask Dame Tell-you-All how to get some, and then how to fly with them.'

'Look—isn't that old Watzisname coming along?' said Joe, suddenly. They looked in the dim distance, and saw that it was indeed Watzisname, looking rather proud. Saucepan was with him, his pans clashing as usual.

'Hi, Watzisname!' called Joe, loudly.

Watzisname came up. 'My name is not Watzisname,' he said a little haughtily. 'I've at last found out what it is. It is an absolutely marvellous name.'

'What is it?' said Beth.

'It is Kollamoolitoomarellipawkyrollo,' said Watzisname, very proudly indeed. 'In future please call me by my real name.'

'Oh dear—I shall never remember that,' said Frannie, and she tried to say it. But she didn't get any further than 'Kollamooli.' Nor did the others.

'No wonder everyone called him "Watzisname",' said Beth to Frannie. 'Watzisname, where are Silky and Moon-Face?'

'My name is not Watzisname,' said Watzisname, patiently. 'I have told you what it is. Please address me correctly in future.'

'He's gone all high-and-mighty,' said Joe. 'Saucepan, WHERE ARE SILKY AND MOON-FACE?'

'Don't know,' said Saucepan, 'and don't shout at me like that. I haven't seen Silky or Moon-Face today.'

'Let's have our picnic here, and then go and see if Silky and Moon-Face have come home,' said Joe. 'Somehow I don't think we'll go about finding out secrets. This land is a bit too mysterious for me!'

But Connie made up her mind she would find a few secrets! She would have a bit of fun on her own.

Connie in Trouble

They all sat down on a flowery bank. It was still twilight, which seemed very odd, as Joe's watch said the time was half past twelve in the middle of the day. As they ate, they watched the different visitors coming and going to the cave on the hillside.

There was an old woman who wanted to ask Witch Know-a-Lot the secret of youth, so that she could become young again, and there was a tiny goblin who had once done a wicked thing, and couldn't forget it. He wanted to know the secret of forgetting, and that is one of the most difficult secrets in the world if you have done something really bad.

The children talked to everyone who passed. It was peculiar, the different secrets that people wanted to know. One grumpy looking pixie wanted to know the secret of laughter.

'I've never laughed in my life,' he told Joe. 'And I'd like to. But nothing ever seems funny to me. Perhaps the Enchanter Wise-Man can tell me. He's very, very clever.'

The Enchanter plainly knew the secret of laughter because, when the grumpy looking pixie came out of the cave he was smiling. He roared with laughter as he passed the picnicking party.

'Such a joke!' he said to them. 'Such a joke!'

'What was the secret?' asked Connie.

'Ah, that's nothing to do with you!' said the pixie. 'That's my secret, not yours!'

The tiny goblin who had once done a wicked thing came up to the children. 'Did you find out the secret of forgetting?' asked Beth.

The goblin nodded.

'I'll tell it to you, because then if you do a wrong thing, maybe you can get right with yourself afterwards,' he said. 'It's so dreadful if you can't. Well, the Wizard Tall-Hat told me that if I can do one hundred really kind deeds to make up for the one very bad one I did, maybe I'll be able to forget a little, and think better of myself. So I'm off to do my first kind deed.'

'Gosh! It'll take him a long time to make up for his one wicked deed,' said Joe. 'Poor little goblin! It must be awful to do something wicked and not be able to forget it. No wonder he looked unhappy.'

A very grand fairy came flying down to the hillside. She looked rich and powerful and very beautiful. Connie wondered what secret she had come to find out. It must be a very grand secret indeed. The fairy did not tell the children what she wanted to know. She smiled at them and went to knock on Mrs Hidden's door.

'Ah! Did you see that fairy?' said Watzisname. 'It would be interesting to know what secret she is after! She has beauty and wealth and power—whatever secret can she want now?'

'What do you think she wants to know, Watzisname?' asked Connie.

'Call me by my proper name and I might tell you,' said Watzisname, haughtily. But Connie couldn't remember it. Nor could the others.

'Well, it isn't going to be much use finding out my real name, if nobody is going to bother to remember it,' said Watzisname, in a huff. 'Saucepan, do you remember my name?'

'Shame? Yes, it is a shame,' said Saucepan.

In the middle of all the explanations to Saucepan as to what Watzisname had really said, Connie slipped away unseen. She was longing to know what secret the beautiful fairy wanted to find out. It must be a very powerful secret. If only she could hear it! Perhaps if she listened outside Mrs Hidden's door, she might catch a few words.

She went off very quietly without being seen, and climbed a little way up the hillside to where she had noticed Mrs Hidden's door.

There it was—a pale green one, striped with red lines and a curious pattern. It was open!

Connie crept up to it. She could hear voices inside. She stood in the doorway and peeped inside. There was a winding passage leading into the hill from the doorway. She crept down it. She turned a corner and found herself looking into a very curious room. It was small, and yet it looked very, very big because when Connie looked at the corners they faded away and weren't there.

It was the same with the ceiling, which Connie felt sure was very low. But when she looked up at it it wasn't there either! There didn't seem to be any end or beginning to the room at all, and yet Connie knew that it was small.

It gave her an uncomfortable feeling, as if she was in a dream. She tried to see Mrs Hidden. She could see the beautiful fairy quite well, and she could hear Mrs Hidden, whoever she was, speaking in a low, deep voice.

But she couldn't see her!

'Oh well, I suppose she's called Mrs Hidden because she is hidden from our sight,' thought Connie. 'I will just hear what she says to the fairy, and then slip away.'

Connie heard the secret that the beautiful fairy wanted to know, and she heard Mrs Hidden give her the answer. Connie shivered with delight. It was a very wonderful and powerful secret. Connie meant to use it herself! She began to creep out of the cave.

But her foot caught against a loose stone in the passage and it made a noise. At once Mrs Hidden called out in a sharp voice: 'Who's there? Who's prying and peeping? Who's listening? I'll put a spell on you, I will! If you have heard any secrets, you will not be able to speak again!'

Connie fled, afraid of having a spell put on her. She came rushing down the hillside, very frightened. The others heard her and frowned.

'Connie! Surely you haven't been after secrets when we said you were not to try and find out anything?' began Joe.

Connie opened her mouth to answer—but not a word came out! Not a single word!

'She can't speak,' said Watzisname. 'She's been listening at doors and hearing things not meant for her ears. I guess old Mrs Hidden has put a spell on her. Serve her right.'

Connie opened her mouth and tried to speak again, pointing back to the cave she had come from. Saucepan got up in a hurry.

'I can see what she means to say,' he said to the others. 'She's been caught prying and peeping, and she's afraid Mrs Hidden will come after her. She probably will as soon as she has finished with that beautiful fairy who went into her cave. We'd better go. Mrs Hidden is not a nice person to deal with when she is angry.'

They all ran to the hole, and got down it as quickly as possible. Connie was so anxious to get away from Mrs Hidden that she almost fell off the topmost branch. Joe caught her just in time.

'Look out!' he said. 'You nearly went headlong down the Tree. Let me go first.'

Connie couldn't answer. Mrs Hidden's spell was clearly very strong. She simply couldn't say a word. It was very unpleasant.

'Hey—do you think Silky and Moon-Face are still up there in the Land of Secrets?' asked Beth. But they weren't, because as they came down the branch to Moon-Face's house, they heard voices, and saw Silky and Moon-Face undoing shopping parcels.

'Oh—so you went shopping, did you?' said Joe. 'We wondered where you were.'

'Yes, we took the little red squirrel shopping and bought him a new sweater,' said Moon-Face. 'He's very pleased. Well, did you go up into the Land of Secrets? Did you find out anything?'

'Yes, we found out Watzisname's real name,' said Joe.

'Oh, good!' said Silky. 'I've always wanted to know it. What is it, Joe?'

Joe wrinkled up his forehead. 'I can't remember,' he said.

'What's the good of a name nobody remembers?' said Watzisname, gloomily. 'It's just stupid.'

'You tell me it, and I'll promise to remember,' said Silky. 'I'll write it down and learn it by heart, Watzisname really I will.'

Watzisname said nothing. Silky gave him a little nudge. 'Go on, Watzisname. Tell me your name—slowly, now, so that I can say it after you.'

Watzisname shook his head, and suddenly looked miserable. 'I—I can't tell you my name,' he said at last. 'I've forgotten it myself! It was such a fine name too. You'll have to call me Watzisname just the same as before. I expect that's why people did begin to call me Watzisname, because nobody could ever remember my real name.'

'Well, it's a pity to think that the only secret we found out has been forgotten already!' said Joe. 'Though I suppose Connie found out a secret she wasn't supposed to know and got punished for it. Moon-Face, Connie can't speak. Isn't it dreadful?'

'Good thing,' said Saucepan, hearing unexpectedly. 'Never says anything really sensible.'

Connie glared at him and opened her mouth to say something back. But no words came.

Silky looked at her in sympathy.

'Poor Connie! Whatever can we do about it? We'll have to wait till the Land of Enchantments comes, and then go up and find someone who can take the spell away. I don't know how to make you better.'

'Why bother?' said Saucepan, annoying Connie even more, when she was already angry at being unable to answer him back. 'Why bother? She'll be much nicer if she can't say a word. We won't know she's there!'

'Never mind, Connie,' said Beth, seeing that Connie looked really upset. 'As soon as the Land of Enchantments comes, we'll take you there and have you put right!'

Off to Find Connie's Lost Voice

Mother was surprised and very concerned, to find that Connie couldn't speak.

'We'd better take her to the doctor,' she said.

'Oh no, Mother, that's no use,' said Joe. 'It's a spell that Mrs Hidden put on Connie for hearing something she shouldn't have listened to. Only another spell can put her right.'

'When the Land of Enchantments comes we will take Connie there, and see if we can find someone who will give her her voice back again,' said Beth.

'She'll have to be patient till then,' said Frannie.

But Connie wasn't patient. She kept opening her mouth to try and speak, but she couldn't say a word.

'Connie shouldn't be so curious,' said Joe. 'It's her own fault she's like this. Perhaps it will teach her a lesson.'

Three days went by, and no news came from the Tree folk. Then old Mrs Saucepan arrived, with a basket full of lovely new-made cakes for them.

'I have heard so much about you,' she said to their mother, smiling all over her rosy-cheeked face. 'I felt I must come and call on you, and bring you a few of my cakes. I have started a shop up the Tree, near Dame Washalot, and I'd be so pleased if you'd try some of my cakes.'

'Stop and have a drink with us, and we'll try your cakes,' said Mother at once. She like the little old lady very much. So Mrs Saucepan stopped and had a drink. She shook her head when she saw that Connie still couldn't speak.

'A pity,' she said. 'A great pity. It just doesn't do to poke your nose into other people's affairs. I hope the poor child will be put right soon. The Land of Enchantments will be at the top of the Tree tomorrow.'

Everyone sat up. 'What, so soon?' said Joe. 'That's a bit of luck for Connie.'

'It is,' said old Mrs Saucepan. 'Still, there are plenty of lands where she might get her voice put right. You'll have to be a bit careful in the Land of Enchantments, though. It's so easy to get enchanted there, without knowing it.'

'Whatever do you mean?' said Mother, in alarm. 'I don't think I want the children to go there, if there is any danger.'

'I'll send Saucepan with them,' said the old lady. 'I'll give him a powerful spell, which will get anyone out of an enchantment if they get into it by mistake. You needn't worry.'

'Oh, that's all right then,' said Joe. 'I didn't want to get enchanted, and have to stay up there for the rest of my life!'

'You must remember one or two things,' said Mrs

Saucepan. 'Don't step into a ring drawn on the ground in chalk. Don't stroke any black cats with green eyes. And don't be rude to anyone at all.'

'We'll remember,' said Joe. 'Thank you very much. Will you tell Saucepan we'll be up the Tree tomorrow, please?'

Old Mrs Saucepan left after they had all had a drink and eaten some of her delicious cakes. She had made firm friends with Mother, who promised to send the children once a week to buy her cakes.

'We'll go to the Land of Enchantments tomorrow,' said Joe. 'Cheer up, Connie—you'll soon get your voice back!'

The next day it was raining, and Mother didn't want the children to go up the Tree. But Connie's eyes filled with tears, and Mother saw how badly she wanted to go.

'Well, put on your raincoats,' she said, 'and take umbrellas. Then you'll be all right. It may not be raining in the Land of Enchantments. And do remember what Mrs Saucepan said, Joe, and be very careful.'

'We'll be careful,' said Joe, putting on his old raincoat. 'No treading in chalk rings—no stroking of black cats with green eyes—and no rudeness from anyone!'

Off they went. The Tree was very slippery to climb, because it was so wet. Somebody had run a thick rope all the way down it, and the children were glad to hold on to it as they went up the Tree. The Angry Pixie was in a bad temper that morning because the rain had come in at his window and made puddles on the floor. He was scooping up the water and throwing it out of the window.

'Look out!' said Joe. 'Go round the other side of the

Tree. The Angry Pixie's in a bad mood.'

Silky was not at home. Dame Washalot, for a change, was not doing any washing, because it really was too wet to dry it. So she was helping Mrs Saucepan to bake cakes on her little stove inside the Tree. The children got a fresh cake each.

Saucepan and Silky were at Moon-Face's house waiting for the children to come.

'Where's Watzisname?' said Joe.

'Gone to sleep,' said Moon-Face. 'Didn't you see him on the way up? Oh no—he would be indoors on a day like this, of course. He sat up half the night trying to remember his real name and write it down so that he wouldn't forget it again. So he was very sleepy this morning. And he didn't remember his name of course.'

'Is the Land of Enchantments up there?' said Joe, nodding his head towards the top of the Tree.

'It must be,' said Silky. 'I've met two witches and two enchanters coming down the Tree today. They don't live here, so they must have come down from the Land of Enchantments.'

'They come down to get the scarlet-spotted toadstools that grow in the Enchanted Wood,' said Saucepan. 'They are very magic, you know, and can be used in hundreds of spells.'

'There goes an old wizard or enchanter now,' said Silky, as someone in a tall pointed hat went down past Moon-Face's door. 'Shall we go now? I'm sure Connie will be glad to get her voice back.'

Connie nodded. But she suddenly remembered what Mrs Saucepan had said—that she would give Saucepan a very powerful spell, so that if any of them got caught in an enchantment, Saucepan could set them free by using his spell.

But she couldn't say all this, of course. So she pulled out the note book she had been using for messages and scribbled something on one of the pages. She showed it to Joe.

'What about the spell that Saucepan was going to take with him?'

'Oh, goodness, yes,' said Joe, and he turned to Saucepan. 'Did your mother give you a powerful spell to take with you, Saucepan, in case we get caught in an enchantment?'

'Uh-Oh!' groaned Saucepan, beginning to look all round him in a hurry. 'Where did I put it? Silky, have you seen it? What did I do with it?'

'You really are a silly, Saucepan,' said Silky, looking everywhere. 'You know it's a spell that can move about. It's no use putting it down for a minute, because it will only move off somewhere.'

The spell was found at last. It was a funny round red spell, with little things that stuck out all round it rather like spiders' legs. It could move about with these, and had walked off Moon-Face's shelf, and settled itself down at the edge of the slippery-slip.

'Look at that!' said Saucepan, snatching it up quickly. 'Another inch and it would have been down the slippery-slip and gone for ever. Where shall I put it for safety?'

'In a kettle and put the lid on,' said Joe. So into a kettle went the spell, and the lid was put on as tightly as could be.

'It's safe now,' said Saucepan. 'Come on, up we go, and be careful, everyone!'

They all left their umbrellas and raincoats behind, and went up into the Land of Enchantments. It wasn't a twilight land like the Land of Secrets; it was a land of strange colours and lights and shadows. Everything shone and shimmered and moved. Nothing stayed the same for more than a moment. It was beautiful and strange.

There were curious little shops everywhere where

'Come on, up we go!'

125

witches, enchanters and goblins cried their wares. There was a shining palace that looked as if it was made of glass, and towered up into the sky. The Enchanter Mighty-One lived there. He was head of the whole land.

There were magic cloaks for sale, that could make anyone invisible at once. How Joe longed to buy one! There were silver wands full of magic. There were enchantments for everything!

'Spell to turn your enemy into a spider,' cried a goblin. 'Spell to enchant a bird to your hand! Spell to understand the whispering of the trees!'

The spells and enchantments were very expensive. Nobody could possibly buy them, for no one in their little group had more than a few coins in their pockets. Even the cheapest spell cost a sack of gold!

'Oh, look at all those fairies dancing in a ring and singing as they dance!' said Beth, turning her head as she saw a party of bright-winged fairies dancing in a ring together.

She went over to watch them, and they smiled at her and held out their hands. 'Come and dance too, little girl!' they cried.

Beth didn't see that they were all dancing inside a ring drawn on the ground in white chalk! In no time she was in the ring too, linking hands with the fairies and dancing round and round!

The others watched, smiling. Then Joe gave a cry of horror, and pointed to the ground.

'Beth's gone into a ring! Beth, come out, quick!'

Beth looked alarmed. She dropped the hands of the fairies, and came to the edge of the ring. But oh dear, poor Beth couldn't jump over it! She was a prisoner in the magic ring.

'Saucepan, get out the spell at once, the one your mother gave you!' cried Joe. 'Quick, quick! Before anything happens to Beth. She may be getting enchanted.'

Saucepan took the lid off the kettle where he had put the spell. He put in his hand and groped around. He groped and he groped, a worried look coming on his face.

'Saucepan, be quick!' said Joe.

'The spell has gone!' said Saucepan miserably. 'Look in the kettle, Joe—the spell isn't there. I can't get Beth out of the magic ring!'

The Land of Enchantments

Everyone stared at Saucepan in horror.

'Saucepan! The spell can't be gone! Why, you put the lid on as tightly as can be,' said Silky. 'Let me look!'

Everyone looked, but it was quite plain to see that the kettle was empty. There was no spell there.

'Well, maybe you didn't put it into that kettle, but into another one,' said Joe. 'You've got so many hanging round you. Look in another kettle, Saucepan.'

So Saucepan looked into every one of his kettles, big and small, and even into his saucepans too—but that spell was not to be found.

'It's really most peculiar,' said Moon-Face, puzzled. 'I don't see how it could possibly have got out! Oh dear, why didn't one of us keep the spell instead of Saucepan? We might have know he would lose it!'

'We're in real danger in this strange land, without a spell to protect us,' said Silky. 'But we can't run off home because we mustn't leave Beth in a magic ring, and we have to try and get Connie put right. Oh dear!'

'We'll have to find someone who will get Beth out of the ring,' said Joe anxiously. 'Let's go round the Land of Enchantments and see if anyone will help us.'

So they started off, leaving poor Beth looking sadly after them. But the fairies took her hands and made her dance once again.

The children came to a small shop where a goblin with green ears and eyes sat at the back. In front of him were piled boxes and bottles of all sorts, some with such strange spells in them that they shimmered as if they were alive.

'Could you help us?' said Joe, politely. 'Our sister has got into a magic ring by mistake, and we want to get her out.'

The goblin grinned. 'Oh, no, I'm not helping you to get her out!' he said. 'Magic rings are one of our little traps to keep people here.'

'You're a very nasty person then,' said Moon-Face, who was upset because he was very fond of Beth.

The goblin glared at him and moved his big green ears backwards and forwards like a dog.

'How dare you call me names?' he said. 'I'll turn you into a voice that can do nothing but call rude names, if you're not careful.'

'Indeed you won't,' said Moon-Face, getting angry. 'What, a silly little goblin like you daring to put a spell on me, Moon-Face! You think too much of yourself, little green goblin. Go and bury yourself in the garden!'

'Moon-Face!' said Frannie, suddenly. 'Don't be rude. Remember what Mrs Saucepan said.'

But it was too late. Moon-Face had been rude and now he was in the goblin's power. When the little green goblin beckoned to him, poor Moon-Face found that his legs took him to the goblin, no matter how he tried not to go.

'You will work for me now, Moon-Face!' said the goblin. 'Now, just sort out those boxes into their right sizes for me. And remember, no more rudeness.'

Frannie burst into tears. She couldn't bear to see Moon-Face having to work for the nasty little goblin. 'Oh, Saucepan, why did you lose that spell?' she wailed. 'Why did you?'

'Here's a powerful looking enchanter,' said Joe, as a tall man in a great flowing cloak swept by. 'Maybe he could help us.'

He stopped the enchanter and spoke to him. A black cat came out from the tall man's shimmering cloak, and strolled over to Silky, blinking its green eyes at her.

'Can you help us, please?' asked Joe, politely. 'Some of our friends are in difficulties here.'

He was just going on to explain, when he suddenly stopped and ran at Silky who was stroking the black cat and saying sweet things to it! She was very fond of cats, and stroked every one she saw. But she mustn't—she mustn't do that in the Land of Enchantments!

It was too late. She had done it. Now she had to follow the enchanter, who smiled at them. 'A nice little fairy!' he said to them. 'I shall like having her around with the black cat. She will be company for him. She can take care of him.'

To the great dismay of the others, the enchanter swept off, taking poor Silky, his cloak flowing out, covering her and the cat.

'Oh, now Silky's gone!' sobbed Frannie. 'First it was

Beth, then Moon-Face, and now Silky. Whatever are we going to do?'

'Look!' said Saucepan, suddenly, and he pointed to a little shop nearby. On it was painted a sentence in yellow paint:

'COME HERE TO GET THINGS YOU HAVE LOST!'

'What about trying to get Connie's voice there,' said Saucepan. 'Not that I want her to have her voice back; I think she's much nicer without it—but we might be able to get it back if we go to that shop.'

They went over to it, Frannie still wiping her eyes. The shop was kept by the same beautiful fairy who had flown to Mrs Hidden's cave, and whose secret Connie had overheard! Connie was afraid of going to her, but Saucepan pulled her over to the shop.

The beautiful fairy knew Saucepan, and was delighted to see him. When he told her about Connie, she looked grave. 'Yes, I know all about it,' she said. 'It was my secret she heard, and a very wonderful secret it was. Has she written it down to tell any of you?'

Connie shook her head. She took out her little note book and wrote in it. She tore out the page and gave it to the fairy.

'I am very sorry for what I did,' the fairy read. 'Please forgive me. I haven't told the secret, and I never will. If you will give me back my lost voice, I promise never to peep and pry again, or to try and overhear things not meant for me.'

'I will forgive you,' said the fairy, gravely. 'But, Connie, if you ever do tell the secret, I am afraid your voice will be lost again and will never come back. Look! I will give it back to you now—but remember to be careful in future.'

She handed Connie a little bottle of blue and yellow liquid, and a small red glass. 'Drink what is in the bottle,' she said. 'Your voice is there. It's a good thing I didn't sell it to anyone.'

Connie poured out the curious liquid and drank it. It tasted bitter, and she pulled a face.

'Oh, how horrid!' she cried, and then clapped her hands in delight. 'I can speak! My voice is back! Oh, I can talk!'

'It's a pity!' said Saucepan. 'I like you better when you don't talk. Still, I needn't listen.'

Connie was so excited at having her voice back again that she talked and talked without stopping. The others were very silent. Both Joe and Saucepan were worried, and Frannie was still crying.

'Be quiet, Connie!' said Joe at last. 'Saucepan, WHAT SHALL WE DO?'

'Go back and ask my mother for another spell,' said Saucepan. 'That's the best thing I can think of.'

So they all went back to the hole in the cloud. But they couldn't get down it because there were so many people coming up!

'The Land of Enchantments must be moving away again soon,' said Saucepan, in dismay. 'Look! Everyone is hurrying back to it, with their toadstools and things!'

'We can't risk going down to your mother then,' said Joe, more worried than ever. 'If the land moves on it will

132

take Moon-Face, Beth and Silky with it, and we shall never see them again.'

They sat down at the edge of the hole, and looked worried and upset. What ever were they going to do?

Then Frannie gave such a loud cry that everyone jumped. 'What's that? What's that sticking out of the spout of that kettle, Saucepan? Something red, waving about—look!'

Everyone looked—and Saucepan gave a shout. 'It's the spell! It must have crawled up the spout, and that's why we didn't see it when we looked in the kettle! It couldn't get out because the spout is too small. Those are its leg-things waving about, trying to get out of the spout!'

'Quick! Get it out, Saucepan,' said Joe.

'Bad spell, naughty spell,' said Saucepan severely, and poked his finger into the spout, pushing the spell right back. It fell with a little thud into the inside of the kettle. At once, Saucepan took off the lid, put it in his hand and grabbed the spell. He jumped to his feet.

'Come on! Maybe we've just got time to rescue the others. Beth first!'

They rushed to the magic ring, and Saucepan stepped into it with the spell held firmly in his hand. At once the chalk ring faded away, the fairies ran off and Beth was free. How she hugged Saucepan!

'No time to waste, no time to waste,' said Saucepan, and ran off to find Silky. He saw the enchanter in his floating cloak, talking to a witch, and rushed up to him.

'Silky, Silky, where are you? I've a spell to set you free!' cried Saucepan.

The enchanter looked down and saw the wriggling red spell in Saucepan's hand. He shook out his cloak and Silky appeared. Saucepan took her by the hand.

'Come on! You're free. You don't need to follow him any more. He's afraid of this spell.'

The enchanter certainly was. He ran off with his black cat without a word.

'Now for Moon-Face,' said Saucepan. 'Gosh, can I hear the humming noise that means this land will soon be on the move?'

He could, and so could the others. With beating hearts, they rushed to the green goblin's shop. There was no time to waste. Saucepan threw the red spell at the goblin, and it went down the back of his neck.

'You're free, Moon-Face. Come quickly!' cried Saucepan. 'The land is on the move!'

Moon-Face rushed after the others, leaving the goblin to try and grab the wriggling spell. Everyone rushed to the hole that led down through the cloud. The land was shaking a little already, as if it was just going to move.

Beth and Frannie were pushed down quickly. Then Silky and Connie followed, almost falling down in their hurry. Then came Moon-Face and Joe, and last of all Saucepan, who nearly got stuck in the hole with his saucepans and kettles. He got free and fell down with a bump.

'The land's just off!' he cried, as a creaking sound came down the ladder. 'We only just escaped this time! Gosh, look how I've dented my kettles!'

What is Wrong with the Faraway Tree?

Connie was very talkative for a few days after they had been to the Land of Enchantments. It seemed as if she had to keep on making sure she had her voice back.

'Well, I half wish you'd lose it again,' said Joe, when Connie had talked for about ten minutes. 'Do let someone else get a word in, Connie!'

'We'll have to take her to the Land of Silence!' said Beth. 'Then she'd be quiet for a bit.'

'What's the Land of Silence?' said Connie, who really loved to hear of all the different lands that came to the top of the Tree.

'I don't know. I only just thought of it,' said Beth, laughing. 'It may not be a land at the top of the Tree for all I know!'

'I wonder what land is there now,' said Connie. 'When are we going to see, Joe?'

'There's no hurry,' said Joe. 'You know Silky and Moon-Face have gone away on holiday for a bit, so they aren't in the Tree. We'll wait till they come back.'

'They'll be back on Thursday,' said Frannie. 'We'll go and see them then. We'll stop and buy some of Mrs

Saucepan's cakes, and take them up to Moon-Face's. Mother, can we go on Thursday?'

'Yes,' said Mother. 'I'll bake some new bread for you to take, too.'

Connie could hardly wait till Thursday came. Joe laughed at her. 'Well, considering that you jeered at the Enchanted Wood, and didn't believe in the Faraway Tree or any of the folk in it, to say nothing of the lands at the top, it's funny that you're keener than any of us to visit there now!' said Joe.

Thursday came. After their dinner the children packed up Mother's lovely new bread, and set off to the Enchanted Wood. They jumped over the ditch and landed in the quiet Wood. The trees were whispering together loudly.

'They seem to be louder than usual,' said Joe. 'They seem sort of excited today. I wonder if anything has happened!'

'Wisha, wisha, wisha,' whispered the trees together, and waved their branches up and down. 'Wisha, wisha, wisha, wisha!'

The children walked to the Faraway Tree. There it was, enormous, its great trunk towering upwards, and its wide-spreading branches waving in the wind.

Joe gave a little cry of surprise.

'What's happening to the Tree? Look, some of its leaves are curling up—sort of withering. Surely it isn't going to shed its leaves yet.'

'Well, it's only summer time,' said Beth, feeling the leaves. 'Don't they feel dry and dead? I wonder what has happened to make them go like this.'

What is Wrong with the Faraway Tree?

'Perhaps the leaves will be all right a bit higher up,' said Connie. 'It's not growing any sort of fruit down here, is it? That's unusual.'

It certainly was. The Faraway Tree as a rule grew all kinds of different fruits all the way up. It might begin with lemons, go on to pears, load itself a bit higher up with peaches, and end up with acorns. You never knew what it would grow, but it certainly grew something.

Now today there was no fruit to be seen, only withering leaves. Joe leapt up on to the first branch. Up he went to the next and the next, but all the way up the leaves seemed to be withering and dying. It was curious and rather alarming. The Faraway Tree was magic— something very serious must be the matter if the leaves were dying.

'That's the first sign that a tree itself is dying, if the leaves wither,' said Joe.

The others looked upset. They loved the Faraway Tree, and all its little Tree folk. It wasn't only a tree, it was a home for lots of little people—and the path to strange adventures far above.

The Angry Pixie was in his room. Joe rapped on the window, and the Pixie picked up a jug of water to throw. But he put it down again when he saw it was Joe.

'Hello!' he said. 'Are you on your way to Moon-Face's? He's just back.'

'Hey, what's the matter with the Faraway Tree?' asked Joe.

The Angry Pixie shook his head gloomily.

'Don't know,' he said. 'Nobody knows. Nobody at all.

It's a very serious thing. Why, the Faraway Tree should live to be a thousand years old—and it's only five hundred and fifty three so far.'

The Owl was asleep in his bed. No water came down from Dame Washalot. When the children got up as far as her branch, they saw her talking seriously to old Mrs Saucepan, who was busy arranging stacks of new made cakes on her stall.

'Can't think what's the matter,' Dame Washalot was saying. 'I've been here on this branch for nearly a hundred years, and never—no, never—have I known one single leaf wither. Why, the tree grows new ones each day, and fruit, too. Many's the time I've stripped this branch of fruit, and before I've cooked it, it has been full again of some other kind of fruit. Now there's none to be seen.'

'What do you think is the matter?' asked Joe, climbing up. But neither of the old women knew. Mister Watzisname was looking carefully at every curled up, withering leaf, to see if caterpillars were the cause of the trouble.

'I thought if it was caterpillars I'd send a call to all the birds in the Enchanted Wood,' he said.

'They would soon put things right, by eating the grubs. But it isn't caterpillars.'

The children went on to Moon-Face's. He was in his curved room with Silky. But he didn't beam at them as usual as he opened his door. He looked anxious and sad.

'Hello!' he said. 'How nice to see you! We've just got back—and what a shock we got when we saw the Tree! I believe it's dying.'

What is Wrong with the Faraway Tree?

'Oh no!' said Joe, quite shocked. 'It's a magic tree, surely?'

'Yes, but even magic trees die if something goes wrong with them,' said Moon-Face. 'The thing is—no one knows what's wrong, you see. We might put it right, if we knew.'

'Do you think the roots want water?' asked Beth. Moon-Face shook his head.

'No—it's been a wet summer, and besides the Tree's roots go down very, very, deep—right into some old caves deep down below. Jewels were once found there, but I don't think there are any now.'

'You know,' said Joe, looking serious, 'my father once had a lovely apple tree that suddenly went like this, all its leaves curling up. I remember quite well.'

'What was the matter with it?' said Silky.

'There was something wrong with its roots,' said Joe. 'I don't know what. But I know my father said that when a tree's roots go wrong, the tree dies unless you can put the trouble right.'

'But what could go wrong with the Faraway Tree's roots?' said Moon-Face, puzzled.

'Could there be anyone down there, interfering with them?' said Joe.

Moon-Face shook his head. 'I shouldn't think so. No one is allowed at the roots, you know. Those old jewel-caves were closed up as soon as the Tree's roots reached to them.'

'Still—it would be a good idea to find out if anything is damaging the roots,' said Joe. 'Could you send a rabbit down, do you think? He could tell you, couldn't he?'

'Yes. That's quite a good idea,' said Moon-Face. He went to the door and whistled for the red squirrel. When the little squirrel came, Moon-Face told him to fetch one of the rabbits that lived in the wood.

One soon came bounding up the Tree like the squirrel! It was odd to watch him. He was pleased to help Moon-Face.

'Listen, Woffles!' said Moon-Face, who knew every single rabbit in the Enchanted Wood. 'Do you know your way down to the jewel-caves at the roots of the Faraway Tree?'

'Of course,' said Woffles. 'But the caves are closed, Moon-Face. They have been for years.'

'Well, we think something may be damaging the roots of the Tree,' said Moon-Face. 'We want you to go down as far as you can, and see if there is anything to find out. Come back and tell us as soon as you can.'

'Could I please go down the slippery-slip, just once?' said the rabbit, shyly.

'Of course,' said Moon-Face, and threw him a cushion. 'There you are. Give it back to the red squirrel at the foot of the Tree.'

The rabbit shot off down the slippery-slip, squealing with excitement and delight.

'Isn't he sweet?' said Frannie. 'I wish he was mine! I hope it won't be long before he's back. Shall we have lunch, Moon-Face? We've brought some new bread from Mother, and some cakes from Mrs Saucepan.'

They began their meal. Before they had finished the rabbit was back, looking very scared.

What is Wrong with the Faraway Tree?

'Moon-Face! Oh, Moon-Face! Look at my bobtail! Half the hairs are gone!'

'What's happened to it?' asked Moon-Face.

'Well, I went down to the old jewel-caves, and I heard a hammering and banging noise,' said the rabbit. 'I burrowed a hole to see what the noise was—and guess what, all the caves are filled with little people! I don't know who they are. They saw me and one caught hold of my tail and nearly pulled all the hairs out.'

Everyone sat silent, staring from one to the other. People in the old jewel-caves—hammering and crashing round the roots of the Faraway Tree! No wonder it was dying. Maybe the roots were badly damaged!

'We'll have to look into this,' said Moon-Face at last. 'Thank you, Woffles. Your hairs will grow again. Red Squirrel, go down the Tree and tell everyone to come up here. We must hold a meeting. Something has got to be done!'

Down to the Jewel-Caves

The red squirrel bounded off down the Tree to call everyone to a meeting. 'Go up to Moon-Face's,' he told everyone. 'There is to be an important meeting about the Faraway Tree. Most important.'

Soon everyone was on their way up the Tree to Moon-Face's house at the top. Dame Washalot arrived, panting. Behind her came old Mrs Saucepan. Mister Watzisname came, and Saucepan too. The Owl came with two friends. The woodpecker came, and two or three squirrels, with a good many baby squirrels to join in the excitement. The Angry Pixie came too, of course.

It was too much of a squash in Moon-Face's curved room, so everyone sat outside on the broad branch. Moon-Face addressed the meeting.

'Something very serious is happening,' he said. 'The Faraway Tree is dying, as you can all see for yourselves. Even in the last hour or two its leaves have curled up even more. And not a single fruit or berry of any kind is to be found from top to bottom, a thing that has never happened before.'

'That's true,' said Dame Washalot. 'I've always depended on the Tree for my pies. But now there isn't any fruit, not even a raisin.'

Down to the Jewel-Caves

'We have discovered that there are people in the jewel-caves at the roots of the Tree,' said Moon-Face, solemnly.

'Oooooh-ooooh!' said everyone, in amazement.

'Woffles went down and saw them,' said Moon-Face. The little rabbit almost fell off the branch with pride when his name was mentioned.

'But—the jewel-caves have been closed for many years!' said Dame Washalot in surprise.

'Yes—because the roots of the Tree went deep into them,' said Moon-Face. 'Anyway, I don't think there were any more jewels to be found. But certainly, there are robbers who think there may be some left, and they have come after them, forced open the caves, and are damaging the roots of the Tree in their hunt for jewels. Unless we can stop them quickly, I am afraid the Faraway Tree will die.'

'Oh dear, would it have to be chopped down?' said Beth in dismay. She couldn't bear to think of such a thing. It would be dreadful. All the children were as fond of the friendly Faraway Tree as the Tree folk were themselves.

'What are we going to do about it?' said the Angry Pixie. 'I wish I could get at those robbers!'

'We'd better find out who they are first. And how many of them,' said Silky. 'Then we could send a message round the Enchanted Wood and get lots of people to come and help us to force the robbers out of the caves. Maybe if we could stop them damaging the roots any more the Tree would recover.'

'I will go down to the jewel-caves myself and speak

with the robbers,' said Moon-Face, his round face looking sad. 'Saucepan, will you come with me?'

'Oh yes. Of course. Without a doubt,' said old Saucepan at once.

'I'm coming too,' said Watzisname.

'And all of us are,' said the children at once, and Silky nodded as well. This looked like a very unpleasant kind of adventure, but they meant to share it as usual.

'Well, I think we should go right away,' said Moon-Face, getting up. 'No time like the present. Coming, all of you?'

'Yes,' said everyone, and stood up. Connie was thrilled. What adventures she had had since she came to stay with Joe, Beth and Frannie!

'Where's Woffles?' said Moon-Face, looking round. 'Ah, there you are! Woffles, please lead the way.'

Woffles proudly ran down the Tree in front of the others. Everyone followed. When they came to the ground Woffles ran to a big rabbit hole.

'Down here,' he said. So down went the children and the four Tree folk, down down into the darkness. It was a good thing the rabbit hole was so big. Rabbit burrows in the Enchanted Wood were always on the large side because the goblins, gnomes, pixies and elves liked to use the underground tunnels when it rained.

'I've never been down a rabbit hole before,' said Connie. 'Never! It's like a dream! I hope I won't wake up and find it isn't real. I like this sort of thing.'

So did the others. It was peculiar down the rabbit hole, rather dark, and a bit musty. Woffles knew the way very well, of course. He knew every burrow in the Wood!

Down to the Jewel-Caves

Here and there were strange lanterns hanging from the roof where it was a bit higher than usual, usually at sharp corners. It was a bit of a squash when anyone else came along in the opposite direction, for then everyone had to flatten themselves against the wall of the tunnel.

Quite a lot of people met them. Rabbits, of course, and elves and goblins seemed to be hurrying about by the hundred.

'Woffles, are you sure this is the way?' said Moon-Face at last, when it seemed as if they had been wandering along dark tunnels for miles and miles. 'Are you sure you are not lost?'

Woffles made rather a rude snort. 'Lost! As if any rabbit is ever lost underground!' he said. 'No, Moon-Face, you can trust me. I never get lost here. I am taking you the shortest way.'

They went on again, feeling their way along the tunnels, glad of an unexpected ray of light from a lantern now and again. And then they heard something!

'Listen!' said Moon-Face, stopping so suddenly that Joe bumped right into him. 'Listen! What is that?'

Everyone stood and held their breath—and they heard strange muffled noises coming from the depths of the earth.

'Boom, boom, boom! Boom, boom, boom!'

'That's the people I told you about,' said Woffles importantly. 'We're getting near the jewel-caves.'

Connie felt a bit strange. She held Watzisname's hand tightly.

'Boom, boom, boom!'

'It's the robbers all right,' said Moon-Face, and his

voice echoed strangely down the tunnel. 'Can't you hear their choppers?'

'Is it safe to go on?' said Silky, doubtfully. 'You don't think they'd take us prisoners or anything, do you?'

'I'll go first with Joe,' said Moon-Face, 'and you others can keep back in the shadows, if you like. I don't think the robbers would try to capture us. They would know that a whole army of people would come down from the Enchanted Wood after them, if they did!'

They went forward again, making as little noise as they could. Even old Saucepan hardly made a clank or a clang with his saucepans and kettles.

'Boom, boom, boom!' The sound came nearer still. 'BOOM, BOOM, BOOM!'

'They are certainly working very hard,' said Joe, in a whisper. 'They are using choppers to break down the caves to see if any more precious stones are hidden there. No wonder the Tree is dying. They must be striking the roots every time.'

'There's a root, look!' said Silky, and she pointed to a thick rope-like thing that jutted out into the tunnel, right across their path. It shone strangely in the light of an old lantern that swung from the roof just there.

'Yes, that's a root,' said Moon-Face, climbing over it. 'Be careful of it, all of you!'

So they were very careful, because they didn't want to hurt the Faraway Tree at all. It was being hurt quite enough, as it was, by the robbers.

'Now, here are the caves,' said Woffles, excitedly, as they turned a corner, and came to a great door, studded with iron and brass. 'You can't get through that door. It's locked.'

'How did you get into the caves?' said Moon-Face. 'Oh yes, I remember, you made a burrow. Where is it?'

Woffles pointed to it with his paw. But gosh, out of it pointed something sharp and glittering! Whatever could it be?

Moon-Face stepped up to see. He came back and whispered gravely. 'It's a sharp spear! The robbers certainly don't want anyone to get into the caves again. There are three of these doors, I know, but the robbers will have locked them all — and any rabbit hole will be guarded by them too — with spears!'

'There must be someone holding the spear,' said Joe. 'Let's go and talk to him! Come on, Moon-Face. We'll tell him what we think of robbers who hurt the roots of the dear old Faraway Tree!'

The Rabbits Come to Help

Joe and Moon-Face walked boldly up to the rabbit hole.
It was the one Woffles had made that day, when he had
gone down to inquire into things. It was clear that the
robbers had discovered it and were guarding it.

The shining spear moved a little, and a harsh voice
cried out sharply:

'Who goes there?'

'This is Joe and Moon-Face,' said Moon-Face. 'We
have come to tell you that you are making the Faraway
Tree die, because you are damaging its roots.'

'Pooh!' said the voice, rudely.

Moon-Face felt angry. 'Don't you care whether or
not you kill a tree?' he asked. 'And the Faraway Tree,
too, the finest tree in the world!'

'We don't care a bit,' said the voice. 'Why should we?
We don't live in the Tree. We are Trolls, who live underground. We don't care about trees.'

'Trolls!' said Moon-Face. 'Of course, I might have
guessed it. You live under the ground and work the soil
there to find gold and precious stones, don't you?'

'How clever you are!' said the mocking voice. 'Now
go away, please. You can't get into the caves, nor can you
stop us doing what we want to. There are plenty of

precious stones here still, and until we have found them all, we shall hold these caves against any enemy.'

'You can have all the jewels you like if only you won't hurt the roots of the Tree,' said Moon-Face, desperately.

'We can't help it,' said the voice. 'The roots grow through the walls, and are always getting in our way. We chop them off!'

'Good heavens! No wonder the poor Tree is dying,' said Joe. 'Moon-Face, whatever are we going to do?'

'Good heavens!'

Moon-Face went a little nearer the rabbit hole. Would it be possible to bring a whole army of Wood Folk and force a way down the hole—or even get the rabbits to make more holes? No, it certainly wasn't possible to get down this hole, in any case. Another spear had now appeared, horribly sharp and pointed.

'How did you get into the caves?' shouted Moon-Face, moving back a little. 'The doors were always kept locked, and Pixie Long-Beard had the key.'

'Oh, we stole it from him and got in easily!' said the voice, with a laugh. 'Then we locked the doors on this side, so that no one else could get in. We've been here a week now, and nobody knew till that interfering rabbit came along. Wait till we get him! We'll deal with him all right.'

Woffles fled to the back of the listening party, terrified. 'It's all right,' said Silky, 'we won't let them get you, Woffles. Don't be afraid.'

Moon-Face and Joe went back to the others. 'I don't see what we can do,' whispered Moon-Face. 'All the doors are locked, and we certainly can't get keys to unlock them, for the one Pixie Long-Beard had was the only one that could unlock those cave doors. And the Trolls are guarding that rabbit hole too well for us to get down it. Even at night there will be someone there to guard it.'

'Do you think we could get the rabbits to tunnel silently somewhere else?' said Joe. 'If only they could make a way for us somewhere, we could all pour in and surprise the Trolls.'

'It's about the only thing to do,' said Moon-Face. 'What do you think, Watzisname?'

The Rabbits Come to Help

'I think the same,' said Watzisname. 'If we can get the rabbits to make a really big hole, we could do something to surprise the Trolls. It's the only way we can get into the caves, isn't it?'

'Yes,' said Moon-Face, thoughtfully. 'Well, we'd better get to work at once. Where's Woffles?'

'Here, Moon-Face!' said the rabbit eagerly. 'Here I am. What can I do? I daren't go down that hole I made, so don't ask me to!'

'I won't,' said Moon-Face. 'It was brave of you to go the first time. What I want you to do, Woffles, is to go and round up all the biggest and strongest rabbits in the Wood and get them here. Then we'll set them to work quickly on a burrow that must come up right in the very centre of the jewel-caves. Maybe the robbers won't expect us to force a way there. They will expect us to come through the walls, not under the floor of the caves.'

'Right, Moon-Face!' said the rabbit, and sped off, his white bobtail bobbing up and down as he went down the tunnel.

It was rather dull, waiting for the rabbits to come. The lantern nearby gave only a faint light. Moon-Face told everyone to speak in the lowest of whispers.

'I'm hungry!' whispered Connie.

Watzisname gave a little giggle. 'I've got some Toffee Shocks,' he said. 'Do you like toffees, Connie?'

'Oh yes,' said Connie, pleased. 'What's a Toffee Shock? I've never heard of one before.'

Watzisname was holding out a paper bag to Connie. The others watched. They knew Toffee Shocks, which were very peculiar. As soon as you began to suck a

151

Toffee Shock it grew bigger. It grew and it grew and it grew, till it completely filled your mouth and you couldn't say a word! Then, very suddenly, it burst into nothing, and your mouth was empty.

Connie took two! Gosh, what would happen? One was bad enough, but two Toffee Shocks would give her something to remember!

She popped the toffees into her mouth. Everyone watched her. Beth began to giggle.

Connie sucked hard. 'It's funny,' she thought. 'The more I suck, the bigger they seem to be. Gosh, they're getting enormous!'

They were! They swelled up, as they always did, and filled Connie's mouth completely, so that she couldn't speak or chew! She stared at the others in horror.

'Gug-gug-gug,' said Connie, in fright, her eyes almost falling out of her head. Her cheeks were puffed out with the swollen toffees, and her tongue was squashed at the bottom of her mouth.

Just as she thought she really couldn't bear it for one moment more, the Toffee Shocks exploded, and went to nothing! Connie stood in the greatest surprise. Her mouth was empty. Where had the toffees gone? She hadn't swallowed them.

The others burst into giggles. Connie was really cross. 'What a nasty trick to play on me!' she said to Watzisname, glaring at him.

'Well, you should only have taken one, not two,' said Watzisname, wiping the tears of laughter from his eyes. 'One Toffee Shock is fun, but two must be awful!'

'Sh! Sh!' said Moon-Face. 'Don't let the Trolls know

152

we are still here. They will be on the watch if they think we are.'

'Well, I think it would be a very good thing to stay here and make a noise,' whispered Silky. 'Then the Trolls will guard this hole, and keep their attention on us, which will give the rabbits a chance to burrow unheard.'

'Silky's right,' said Joe. 'We'll talk loudly and make a noise. Then perhaps when the rabbits do their burrowing under the floor of the caves, the Trolls won't notice it.'

So they all began to talk and laugh loudly. A third spear appeared at the entrance of the hole, and a voice said: 'If you are thinking of getting down here, think again!'

'Your spears won't stop us when we charge down that hole!' yelled Moon-Face, which made a fourth spear appear, shining brightly.

In a little while a whole army of rabbits appeared at the back of the passage, jostling one another, headed by Woffles, who was bursting with pride again. 'I've brought them,' he said. 'Here they all are, the biggest and strongest.'

Moon-Face told them what he wanted them to do. 'We want you to make a passage right under the caves,' he said, 'so that it comes up in the floor. The Trolls won't be expecting that. Whilst you're doing it, I'll send a message to the pixies in the Wood to come, and help us to burst through the tunnel you make as soon as it is finished.'

As the rabbits began to burrow rapidly downwards,

Moon-Face decided to send Silky, Frannie, Beth and Connie back up the Tree, so they could send out the message to the pixies in the Wood.

'Oh, but we want to see what happens!' said Beth.

'We'll tell you what happens as soon as we know,' promised Joe. 'Silky, can you send a message to the pixies when you get above ground?'

'I will,' said Silky, and she and the three girls made their way back up the burrow and into the Wood. They met a pixie and gave him the message to get a small army together.

The rabbits burrowed quickly and silently down into the earth, down and down and down. When they knew they were right underneath the centre of the jewel-caves, they began to burrow up again, up and up and up. They meant to come up just in the middle of the floor of the centre cave.

Pixies poured down into the tunnel. Everyone followed the rabbits closely, meaning to rush the caves as soon as the tunnel broke through the floor.

But it was not to be! When the rabbits had burrowed upwards to the caves, they came to a stop. Something hard and solid was above them. They couldn't burrow into it.

'What is it?' whispered Moon-Face anxiously. 'Let me feel.' He felt. 'It's heavy blocks of stone!' he groaned. 'Of course, the floor of the caves is paved with stone. I had forgotten that. We can't possibly get through. I'm so sorry, rabbits—all your work has been for nothing!'

'Ha, ha, ho, ho!' suddenly came the distant sound of

laughter. 'We heard you burrowing! You didn't know the floors were made of stone! Ha ha, ho ho!'

'Horrid Trolls!' said Moon-Face, as they all made their way back down the tunnel. 'What can we do now?'

The Land of Know-Alls

'We'd better get back up the Tree, and tell Silky and the others we've failed,' said Moon-Face, gloomily. 'It looks to me as if the poor old Faraway Tree is done for. It's very, very sad.'

They all went back up the Tree, and the pixies returned to their homes in the Wood. Silky and the girls were very upset to hear that the rabbits hadn't been able to get through the floors of the caves.

'Heavy stone there,' said Joe. 'No one could burrow through that, or even move it. It's bad luck. There's no other way of getting down to the caves at all.'

Everyone sat and thought. Nobody could think of any plan at all. 'It isn't that we're stupid,' said Moon-Face. 'It's just that it's impossible.'

'I suppose we couldn't ask anyone in the Land of Know-Alls for help, could we?' said Dame Washalot, at last.

'The Land of Know-Alls! Is that up at the top of the Tree now?' said Moon-Face, looking excited.

'Yes. Didn't you know?' said Dame Washalot. 'I went up there this morning to find out how to do my washing in cold water, when I can't get enough hot. I found out all right, too. There's nothing they don't know up there!'

The Land of Know-Alls

'Goodness! Perhaps they know how to get down into the caves then!' said Moon-Face. 'Or maybe they could give us a key to open the doors.'

'That wouldn't be much use,' said Joe. 'You can be sure the Trolls have put guards at the doors in case we thought of that. They are well armed too. It is only by taking them completely by surprise that we could defeat them.'

'That's true,' said Moon-Face. 'Well, what about going up into the Land of Know-Alls? We might get some good advice. There are only five Know-Alls, and between them they know everything.'

'Oh, do let's go now, this very minute!' said Connie, impatiently.

'All right, we will,' said Joe, and he got up.

'I'll go and finish my washing,' said Dame Washalot. 'And you had better see if your cakes are burning, Mrs Saucepan. You left some in the oven.'

'My goodness, so I did,' said old Mrs Saucepan, and climbed quickly down the Tree.

The rest of them wanted to go into the Land of Know-Alls, even the Angry Pixie, who didn't often go into any of the strange lands.

They all went up the topmost branch and climbed up the yellow ladder through the cloud. They came out into the Land of Know-Alls.

It was a small land, so small that it looked as if anyone could fall off the edge quite easily here and there. In the very middle of it, on a steep hill, rose a magnificent glittering palace, with so many thousands of windows that it looked like one big shining diamond.

From the middle of the palace rose a tremendously tall tower.

The children and the others went up two hundred steps to the great front door. Then they saw about a thousand attendants lining the hall inside, all dressed in blue and silver. They all bowed to the little company at once, looking like a blue and silver cornfield blown by the wind, so gracefully did they bow at the same moment together.

'What is your wish?' said the thousand attendants, sounding like the wind whispering.

'We want to see the Know-Alls,' said Moon-Face.

'They are in the Tall Tower,' said the attendants. Then a hundred of them took the little party to what looked like a small room, but which was really a lift. Ninety-nine attendants bowed them in. One got in with them and pulled a silver rope. The children and the others gasped as the lift shot up the tower. It went so fast. Up and up and up it went, till the children thought they would land on the moon!

At last the lift slowed down and stopped. The door slid open. The children saw that they had come to the top of the Tall Tower. It was surrounded on all sides by wide windows, and the children gasped again as they looked out. It looked as if they could see the whole world from those windows! Oceans, seas, lands spread out on each side of them, and lay glittering in the brightest sunlight they had ever known.

Then they saw the five Know-Alls. They were strange, wonderful and peculiar folk, so old that they had forgotten their youth, so wise that they knew everything.

The Land of Know-Alls

Only their calm, mysterious eyes moved in their old, old faces. One of them spoke, and his voice came from very far away—or so it seemed.

'You have come to ask for advice. You want to know how to get into the jewel-caves?'

'How does he know?' whispered Connie to Joe in amazement.

'Well, he is a Know-All,' said Joe. 'Sh! Don't talk now. Listen!'

Moon-Face stood before the wise Know-All, and spoke to him. 'The Faraway Tree is dying. It is because there are Trolls in the jewel-caves underground, cutting the roots that give the great Tree its life. How, please Know-All, can we get down to the caves and stop them?'

The wise Know-All shut his gleaming, mysterious eyes as if he was thinking or remembering something. He opened them again and looked at Moon-Face.

'There is only one way. Your slippery-slip goes to the foot of the Tree, down its centre. Bore down still further, from your slippery-slip, and you will come out at last right under the tree, in the centre of its tangled roots. Then you can surprise the Trolls and overcome them.'

Everyone looked thrilled. Of course! If only they could make the slippery-slip go deeper down and down and down, they would come out in the middle of the roots! It was a marvellous idea.

'Thank you so much, wise Know-All,' said Moon-Face. 'Thank you! We will go straight away and follow your advice!'

The little group of friends bowed to the five strange

Know-Alls, with their calm, mysterious eyes. Then they stepped into the lift, and the little attendant pulled on the silver rope.

'Oh!' gasped everyone as the lift moved swiftly downwards. It really seemed as if it was falling! It slowed down at last, and the children and everyone else walked out into the vast hall.

Down the steps they went, and back to the hole in the cloud, feeling excited and a little strange. The five Know-Alls always made people feel strange.

'Well,' said Moon-Face, when they were safely in his curved room, and were beginning to feel a little more ordinary. 'Well, now we know what to do. The next thing is—how do we bore a hole down through the rest of the Tree to its roots? I haven't any tools big enough to do that.'

'You know,' said Silky, suddenly, 'you know, Moon-Face, there is a caterpillar belonging to a goat-moth, that bores tunnels in the trunks of trees. I know, because I've seen one. It had made quite a burrow in the wood of the tree, and it lived there by itself till it was time to come out and turn into a chrysalis. Then, of course, it changed into a big goat-moth.'

'Surely you don't think that a little caterpillar could burrow down this big tree!' said Joe.

'Well, if Moon-Face could get about twelve of these goat-moth caterpillars, and could make them ever so much bigger, they could easily eat their way down, and make way for us,' said Silky.

Moon-Face slapped his knee hard and made everyone jump. 'Silky's got the right idea!' he said. 'That's just what we will do! We can easily make the caterpillars large. Then they can burrow down fast. Silky, you're really very clever.'

Silky blushed. It wasn't often she had better ideas than Moon-Face, but this time she really had thought of something good.

'Now we'll have to find out where any goat-moth caterpillars are,' said Moon-Face. 'What tree do they usually burrow in, Silky?'

'There is one in the big elm tree, and two or three in the willows by the stream, and some in the poplars at the other side of the wood,' said Silky. 'I'll go and get them, if you like. They smell a bit horrid, you know.'

'Yes, like goats, don't they?' said Watzisname. 'They're funny creatures. They live for three years in the trunks of trees, eating the wood! Funny taste, some creatures have. Go and get some, Silky. Take a box with you.'

Silky sped off on her errand, taking a big box from Moon-Face's curved cupboard. Joe looked at the time.

'I really think we should go, Moon-Face,' he said. 'It's getting very late. I suppose Silky will bring back the caterpillars soon, and you'll make them enormous and set them to work tonight? We'll come back tomorrow morning and see how you are getting on.'

'I shall rub the caterpillars with growing magic when Silky brings them,' said Moon-Face, 'but it will take them all night to grow to the right size. I shall probably set them to work after breakfast, Joe, so come then.'

Joe and the girls slid down the slippery-slip, shot out of the trap door and made their way home. They were tired, but very thrilled. How they hoped they could defeat those Trolls, and perhaps save the dear old Faraway Tree!

'We'll go back tomorrow, first thing after breakfast,' said Joe. 'I expect old Moon-Face will have worked out some brilliant plan by then. I only hope we punish those bad Trolls properly. Fancy not caring if they killed the Faraway Tree or not!'

'I can hardly wait for tomorrow,' sighed Connie. 'I really don't think I can.' But she had to, of course—and tomorrow came at last, as it always does. What was going to happen then?

A Surprise for the Trolls

Next morning, immediately after an early breakfast, the four children set off to the Faraway Tree. They felt sad when they got near it and saw how much more withered the leaves were.

'It looks almost dead already,' said Joe, miserably. 'I don't believe we can save it, even if we defeat the Trolls today.'

They climbed up. Moon-Face and Silky were waiting for them in the curved room. With them, in the room, were some very peculiar looking creatures—eleven goat-moth caterpillars.

They were great pinkish-coloured caterpillars with black heads. A broad band of chocolate brown ran down their long backs. They were really enormous, like long, fat snakes!

'Hello!' said Moon-Face, beaming round. 'The caterpillars are nearly ready. I rubbed them with the growing magic last night, and they have grown steadily ever since. They are almost ready to go down the slippery-slip now and start eating the wood away at the bottom, to go right down into the roots of the Tree.'

The caterpillars didn't say a word. They just looked

at the children with big solemn eyes, and twitched their many legs.

'I think they're ready,' said Moon-Face. 'Now, Joe, listen! The caterpillars are going to burrow a way for us right through the bottom part of the trunk of the Tree, into the heart of its roots. They are going to crawl out and frighten the Trolls, who will probably run away. Then our job is to rush after them and capture them. All the pixies are ready at the foot of the Tree. They are going to climb in through the trap door, as soon as the caterpillars have gone down into the roots.'

Everyone listened to this long speech, and thought the plan was excellent. Moon-Face gave a cushion to the biggest goat-moth caterpillar, who curled himself up on it. Then off it whizzed down to the foot of the Tree, followed by all the others, one after another.

The children gave the caterpillars a little time to burrow, and then followed them down the slippery-slip. When they got to the trap door they shot out and saw lots of pixies waiting there. Moon-Face climbed back in through the trap door and looked by the light of a lamp to see what had become of the caterpillars.

All he could see was a tunnel eaten out, going down and down into the roots!

'They're going fast!' he said, looking out of the trap door. 'Out of sight already! My word, fancy being able to eat wood like that.'

Soon Moon-Face reported that he thought they might all follow down the way the caterpillars had made. Their strong jaws made easy work of the wood of the Tree, and they were now almost at the bottom, among the roots. It was time to follow them, and help to surprise the Trolls.

Moon-Face, Saucepan, Mister Watzisname, the Angry Pixie, Joe and all the other pixies from the Wood, crept down the hole. Sometimes it was as steep as the slippery-slip, and they slid. It was dark, but everyone was too excited to mind. Silky, Frannie, Beth, Connie and Silky waited impatiently by the trap door. The caterpillars came to the end of the enormous trunk, and found themselves in a tangle of great rope-like roots, going down and down. They crawled among them, with Moon-Face holding on to the tail-end of the last one, so as not to lose the way.

They came out into the very middle of the biggest cave. There was no one there, though the sound of distant hammering or digging could be heard.

'No Trolls to be seen!' whispered Moon-Face to the others. 'Sh! I can hear some coming now!'

Moon-Face and the others slipped back into the tangle of roots, but the great snake-like caterpillars went crawling on. Just as they came to the entrance of the cave, two Trolls came in, almost falling over the caterpillars. They gave a yell.

'Oooh! Snakes! Run, run! Snakes!'

They ran off, screaming. The caterpillars solemnly followed, all eleven of them in a line. They met more Trolls, and every one of them ran away shrieking, for they were really afraid of snakes, and they certainly thought these enormous caterpillars were some dreadful kind of snake!

'After them!' cried Moon-Face, and waving a strong

stick in the air he led the way into the jewel-caves. In one corner was a great pile of glittering jewels. The Trolls had found a fortune down there!

The Trolls were shouting to one another. 'The caves are full of snakes! Hide! Hide!'

The robbers crowded into a cave, put a great stone at the entrance, and pressed against it to prevent the caterpillars from entering. When Moon-Face came up, he lowered his big stick and grinned round at the others.

'Our work is easy! They've shut themselves in, and we can easily make them prisoners!'

'Who's there?' called a Troll, hearing Moon-Face's voice.

'The enemy!' said Moon-Face. 'You are our prisoners. Come out now, and we will keep off the snakes. If you don't give yourselves up, we will push away the stone and let the snakes in!'

Joe giggled. It was funny to think that anyone should be so afraid of caterpillars. The creatures were quite enjoying themselves, crawling round and about, getting in everyone's way.

'We'll come out,' said the Troll's leader, after talking to his men. 'But keep off those snakes!'

'Hold the caterpillars, you others,' whispered Moon-Face. 'Now, all together—heave away the stone!'

The Trolls came out, looking very scared. They were glad to see that the 'snakes' were being held back by Joe and the others. The pixies at once surrounded them, and bound their hands behind their backs.

'We'll keep them in prison till next week, when the Land of Punishment comes back again,' said the head pixie with a grin. 'Then we'll push them all up the ladder, and see that they don't come down. They can move off with the Land of Punishment—it will do them good to live there for the rest of their lives!'

Moon-Face stayed down in the caves whilst the pixies found the key, unlocked the doors and marched out the frightened Trolls. They were strange looking folk, with large heads, small bodies and large limbs.

'Let's have a look round and see what damage has been done to the Tree,' said Moon-Face. 'Just look—see how they've chopped that root in half, and cut this one, and spoilt that one. The poor Tree! No wonder it began to wither and die.'

'What can we do for it?' said Joe, anxiously.

'Well, I've got some wonderful ointment,' said Moon-Face. 'I'm going to rub the damaged roots with it—you can all help—and we'll see if it does any good. It's very magic. I got it out of the Land of Medicines, years ago, and I've still got some left. I hope it's still got magic in it.'

Moon-Face took a little blue pot out of his pocket and removed the lid. It was full of strange green ointment.

'Better send up for the others and let them help too,' said Joe. But just at that moment the girls and Silky came rushing up, led by Woffles. The pixies had told them all that had happened, and they had come down in great delight.

'We're going to rub the damaged roots with magic ointment,' said Moon-Face, and he held out the blue pot. 'Dip your fingers in it, everyone, and hurry up. We

167

can't afford to waste a single moment now, because the poor old Tree is almost dead!'

The children and the others kept dipping their fingers into the pot of ointment, which, in a most magical way, never seemed to get empty. Then, with the green ointment on their fingers, everyone rushed about to find damaged roots. They rubbed the ointment well into the roots, and came back for more.

'Well,' said Moon-Face, after two hours' very hard work, 'shall we take a rest, and go up to see if the Tree is looking any better? I could do with some hot chocolate or something. Let's go and see if old Mrs Saucepan has got some cakes and will make us something to drink.'

So they walked up through the rabbit burrows and then climbed the Tree to Dame Washalot's. To their great disappointment all the leaves were still curled up and withered, and the Faraway Tree looked just as dead as before.

'I suppose the magic ointment isn't any use now,' said Silky, sadly. 'Poor, poor Tree. Moon-Face, will we have to leave it if it dies? Will it be chopped down?'

'Oh, don't talk about such horrid things,' said Moon-Face.

Suddenly Joe gave a shout that made them all jump.

'Look! The leaves are uncurling! The Tree is looking better. It really is!'

It was quite true. One by one the withered leaves were straightening out, uncurling themselves, waving happily in the breeze once more. And then, to everyone's delight, the Tree began to grow its fruits as usual!

A Surprise for the Trolls

Large and juicy oranges appeared on all the nearby branches, and shone in the golden sun. The children put out their hands and picked some. They had never tasted such lovely oranges in their life!

'There are some pineapples just above us, and some raisins just below!' said Connie, in surprise. 'The Tree is doing well, isn't it? I've never seen such a lovely lot of fruit before!'

'The magic ointment has begun its work,' said Silky, happily. 'Now the Faraway Tree will be all right. Thank goodness we found out how to capture those horrid Trolls, and how to cure the poor old Tree!'

Everyone in the Tree rejoiced that day. The folk of the Enchanted Wood came up and down to pick the fruit. Woffles the rabbit came, his eyes shining with pleasure to think he had helped to save the Tree. He was dressed in the red squirrel's old sweater, and was very proud of it.

'He gave it to me as a reward,' said Woffles, proudly. 'Isn't it lovely?'

'Yes, and you look really nice!' said Silky. 'Come and have a drink, you funny little rabbit!'

The Land of Treats

Everyone was very, very glad that the dear old Faraway Tree was all right again. It had been dreadful to think that it was dying, and might have to be chopped down. Now it seemed to be better than ever.

The children visited it every morning to pick the fruit to take home for their mother to make into pies and desserts. Everyone in the Tree was doing the same, and old Mrs Saucepan made quite a lot of money by selling fruit pies to the people who went up and down the Tree.

The bad Trolls, who had damaged the Tree's roots, had all been taken up to the Land of Punishments, which was now at the top of the Tree.

'You should just hear the shouts and yells that those bad Trolls make up there,' said Moon-Face with a grin, to the children. 'They're having a bad time. They keep on trying to escape, and get down the ladder, but they can't.'

'Why can't they?' asked Joe.

'Look and see,' said Moon-Face, with a wider grin than before.

So Joe climbed up the topmost bough, and got on to the bottom rung of the ladder. He couldn't go any further because on the other rungs were the goat-moth caterpillars, still enormous! There they were curled, like enormous snakes, waiting for the Trolls to try and escape.

'The Trolls are very scared of them,' called up Moon-Face, 'and as soon as they see them, they rush back into the Land of Punishment. They don't know which is worse, snakes or punishment!'

The others giggled. 'What are you going to do with the caterpillars when the Land of Punishment has moved on?' asked Beth.

'Oh, change them back to their right size again and take them to the trees we got them from,' said Silky. 'Right now, they are having pies and cakes to eat, instead of the wood they like, but we'd need to give them trees to gnaw if we fed them properly, they're big now! Still, they seem to like the pies.'

'How long is this land going to stay?' asked Connie, suddenly. 'I hope it won't stay too long, because I've got to go home soon. Mother's better and she's coming back, so I've got to go too. I don't want to, because it's such fun here.'

'Well, you should be glad your mother is better and ready to take you home,' said Joe. 'You're a selfish little girl, Connie!'

'All the same, it has been such fun here,' said Connie.
'You'd hate to leave the Enchanted Wood and the Faraway Tree and Moon-Face and Silky and the rest of your friends, you know you would!'

'Yes, we would,' said Beth. 'Moon-Face, I wish a really nice land could come before Connie goes—just

for a treat for her, you know. Something like the Land
of Birthdays, or the Land of Take-What-You-Please—or
the Land of Goodies! That was lovely! Connie, some
of the houses in the Land of Goodies were made of
chocolate!'

'Oooh—how lovely!' said Connie. 'Moon-Face, what
land is coming next?'

'Well, I think it's the Land of Treats, but I'm not
quite sure,' said Moon-Face. 'I'll find out and let you
know.'

'The Land of Treats! What's that like?' said Connie,
thinking that it sounded fine.

'Well, it's full of treats,' said Moon-Face; 'you
know—donkey rides, presents, Christmas trees and ice-
creams, and things like that.'

'And parties, and musicals and balloons and . . .'
went on Silky.

'Gosh!' said Connie, her eyes shining. 'What a lovely
land that would be to visit for my last one. Oh, I do hope
it comes before I go!'

It did. Two or three days after that, the red squirrel,
dressed in his new sweater, arrived at the children's
cottage with a message.

He knocked on the window, and made Mother jump.
But when she saw it was the squirrel, she opened the
window and let him in. She was getting quite used to the
children's strange friends now.

'Joe! Beth! Here's the red squirrel!' she called, and
the children came running in.

'Good morning!' said the squirrel, politely. 'I've
come with a message from Moon-Face, and Moon-Face

says that the Land of Treats will be at the top of the Tree tomorrow, and are you coming?'

'Of course!' cried the children, in delight, 'Tell Moon-Face we'll be there.'

'I will,' said the squirrel and bounded off.

The next day the four children all went up the Tree in excitement. A rope had again been run down through the branches, for hundreds of the Wood folk were going up to the Land of Treats. Whenever a really nice land was at the top, the Tree had plenty of traffic up and down!

Moon-Face, Silky, Watzisname and Saucepan were waiting for them impatiently. 'There are elephants,' said Silky, 'They give you rides. I'm going on an elephant.'

'And you can go up in a balloon,' said Moon-Face. 'Can't you, Saucepan?'

'Moon? Go to the moon? Can you really?' said Saucepan, looking excited.

'UP IN A BALLOON!' yelled everyone, and Saucepan looked startled.

'All right, all right! No need to shout,' he said. 'Come on, let's go now. I want a treat.'

The Old Saucepan Man led the way up the topmost branch. The others followed. Soon they all stood in the Land of Treats.

It looked absolutely lovely. Near them was a large size roundabout, with animals to ride—and they were magic animals who sometimes came alive!

'Oh, let's go on the roundabout!' said Connie.

'No, let's get ice-creams first,' said Joe. 'Look at these! Did you ever see such beauties?'

The ice-cream man was standing with his little van, handing out ice-creams for nothing. They were enormous, and you could have any flavour you liked.

'You've only got to say 'chocolate!' or 'lemon!' or 'pineapple!' and the man just dips his hand in and brings you out the right kind,' said Moon-Face, happily.

'He can't have got every flavour there,' said Connie. 'I'll ask for something he won't have and see what happens.'

So when her turn came she said solemnly, 'I want a fish ice-cream please.'

And hey presto! The ice cream man just as solemnly handed her out a large ice-cream which was quite obviously made of fish because the others could see a few fish bones sticking out of it!

'Ha, ha, Connie! Serves you right!' said Joe.

Connie looked at the ice-cream and wrinkled up her nose. She handed it to the ice-cream man, and said 'I won't have this. I'll have a strawberry one, please.'

'Have to eat that one first, dear,' said the ice-cream man. So Connie had to go without her ice-cream, because she didn't like the taste of the fish one, and couldn't eat it. She gave it to a cat who came wandering by looking for his treat, which he hoped would be fish!

'Now let's go on the roundabout,' said Joe, when he had finished his ice-cream. 'Come on! I'm going on that giraffe.'

'I shall have a lion,' said Moon-Face, bravely. 'I'll have that one. It has such a wonderful mane.'

Connie didn't feel like a lion or a giraffe. She thought she would choose an animal who might be a

174

pet. So she chose a nice tabby cat, who stood waiting for someone to climb on her back.

'Take your seats please!' called the roundabout man, a very amusing man who turned himself round and round and round all the time his roundabout was going, and only stopped when the roundabout stopped too.

Frannie chose a duck that had the softest back she had ever sat on! Beth liked the look of a brown bear. Silky chose a hen. Saucepan chose a large mouse, and Watzisname took a dog with a waggy tail.

The roundabout music began to play. The roundabout moved on its way, round and round and round, going faster and faster. The animals came alive and real, and Saucepan made his mouse move over to Connie, meaning to ask her how she was enjoying such a treat.

But this was a great mistake, because Connie was riding a cat. The roundabout man always put the mouse on the opposite side to the cat, and now here was the mouse almost under the cat's nose!

The cat gave an excited mew when it smelt the mouse. It shot out its paw, and the mouse squealed in fright. It leapt right off the roundabout, and Saucepan almost fell off. He clung to the large mouse, all his pans rattling and clanging.

The cat rushed off the roundabout after the mouse. The roundabout man gave a yell and stopped the roundabout. The children leapt off and stared at Connie and the cat chasing Saucepan and the mouse!

'Gosh! I hope the cat doesn't eat old Saucepan as well as the mouse!' groaned Moon-Face.

Goodbye to the Faraway Tree

Everyone in the Land of Treats stood and watched Connie's cat chasing Saucepan's mouse. Round and round and in and out they went, knocking over stalls of fruit and upsetting all kinds of little folk.

The mouse ran into a hole in the ground, and Saucepan fell off with a crash. He stood in front of the hole and clashed a kettle and saucepan together, frightening the cat, who stopped so suddenly that Connie shot over its head.

'Now, now, now!' said the roundabout man, panting along, looking very angry. 'Puss, have you forgotten this is the Land of Treats? I shall have to stop you coming alive if you don't behave!'

The cat looked very sorry. 'We shall have to give the mouse a real treat all for himself,' said the roundabout man. 'Go back to the roundabout, Puss. Come out, Mouse, and you will have a treat to make up for your fright.'

The mouse came out, its nose twitching. The roundabout man beckoned to an old woman who was selling sandwiches at a nearby stall.

'Four cheese sandwiches, please,' he said. There you are, Mouse, that's a lovely treat for you!'

The mouse squealed his thanks and took the sandwiches down the hole, in case the cat came back again. The roundabout man frowned at Saucepan.

'You should have known better than to take your mouse over to the cat,' he said. 'I always keep them on opposite sides of my roundabout in case they come alive. Don't do it again, please.'

'Let's come and have a ride in a balloon,' said Moon-Face, seeing that Saucepan looked rather miserable. 'Look! We get into that basket-thing there, and they let the balloon go, and it carries us up in the basket below it.'

So they all got into the basket, and the balloon rose into the air and took them with it. They had a wonderful view of everything.

And then somebody cut the rope! Connie gave a squeal as the balloon rose high, and floated right across the Land of Treats!

'The balloon's flying away! What shall we do?'

'Don't be silly!' said Moon-Face. 'This is all part of the treat. We come down near the boating pool, and choose a boat to go on the water.'

He was quite right. It was all part of the treat. The balloon floated on gently, and came down beside a big blue boating pool, where there were many exciting boats, all in the shape of birds or animals.

'Now, Saucepan, for goodness' sake don't choose that mouse-boat and take it near the cat-boat,' said Moon-Face.

'Come on, Saucepan! We'll share a boat together, then you can't get into trouble,' said Silky.

They hustled him into a boat shaped like a grey-and-white seagull. Joe got into a boat like a goldfish, which sometimes put its head under the water and opened and shut its mouth to breathe. The others all chose boats too, and Connie's was the best, a magnificent peacock! It spread its tail to make a sail, and everyone stared at it in admiration.

Silky's seagull-boat gave her and Saucepan a great surprise, because it suddenly rose into the air, spread its wings and flew around the pool. It came to rest with a little splash, and Silky got out hurriedly. Saucepan

Many exciting boats.

178

stayed in. He liked boats that flew. He was so pleased with the seagull-boat that he presented it with a large-sized saucepan when he did at last get out. The seagull thought it was a hat and put it on proudly.

'Now, what next?' said Joe, when they had all had enough of the boats. 'What about something to eat. There's an exciting place over there, where you can get anything you like, just by pressing a button. Let's try it, shall we?'

So they went to the curious little counter, where a smiling pixie stood. There were buttons all over the counter, which could be pressed. As you pressed them, you said what you wanted, and it came out of a little trap door in the side of the counter.

'I'll have chicken, sausages, and salad,' said Joe, who felt hungry. Moon-Face pressed a button for him, while Joe watched the trap door. It opened, and out came a plate with chicken, sausage and salad on it. Joe took it and went to sit at a nearby table, which was set with knives, forks and spoons.

'What will you have, Silky?' asked Saucepan, who was longing to press a button.

'Pears and cream,' said Silky.

Saucepan pressed a button and spoke loudly. 'Bears and cream!'

Immediately, a plate shot out of the trap door with a little jug of cream—but there were no pears on the plate, instead there were small teddy bears, arranged in rings.

'Oh, Saucepan, I said pears not bears!' cried Silky, and she gave the plate back to the pixie behind the counter. She pressed a button herself, and a plate of

179

juicy pears came out of the trap door. Silky joined Joe at his table.

'I'll have a big chocolate pudding,' said Moon-Face as he pressed a button, and out came the biggest chocolate pudding he had ever seen.

Saucepan pressed a button and got a cherry pie and cucumber sandwiches. He went off to a table by himself to eat them.

Everyone got what they wanted. In fact, they had more than they wanted, because it was such fun to press the buttons and get something else. The buttons were marvellous and they produced anything that anyone asked for. Even when Connie asked for a strawberry cake, stuffed with sausage meat, iced with chocolate, and topped with syrup, the button she pressed made exactly what she wanted come out of the trap door. Connie said it tasted really lovely.

They went over to the circus after that, and had an exciting time, especially when anyone who wanted to could have a ride on a horse. It was lovely to ride around the circus ring, on the back of a beautiful horse.

Then they went into a magician's room and sat down on the floor to watch him do magic tricks. He was the best conjurer anyone had ever seen.

'Ask me what you want, and I will do it!' he cried, after every trick, and then somebody or other would call out something very difficult. But, the magician always managed to do it.

'Make roses come in my kettle!' said Saucepan, and he held out one of his kettles.

'Easy!' said the magician, and tapped the kettle with

his wand. Immediately the smell of roses came into the room. Saucepan took off the lid, and put in his hand. He pulled out lots of deep red velvety roses. He gave one to everyone to wear.

'Make me fly round the room!' cried Connie, who had always longed to fly.

The magician tapped her shoulders, and two long blue wings shot out from them. Connie stood looking over her shoulder at them. Then she flapped them— and to her great joy, she flew into the air as easily as a butterfly, hovering here and there as light as a feather.

'Oh, oh! This is the greatest treat I've ever had!' she cried, and flew round once again. Then, as she came to the ground, the magician tapped her once again and the wings disappeared. Connie was disappointed. She had hoped she would be able to keep them. She wouldn't have minded going back home, if only she could have taken her wings with her.

The magician took a couple of goldfish out of Joe's ears. 'What a place to keep goldfish!' he said. 'You should keep them in an aquarium.'

'But . . . but,' began Joe in surprise.

The magician took an empty aquarium from the top of Silky's head, made Joe lean over sideways, and filled the aquarium with water that seemed to come out of Joe's ear. He gave the goldfish to Joe.

'Now don't you keep those goldfish in your ears any more,' he said. 'You keep them in that!'

Everyone laughed at Joe's astonished face.

'I'll take them home to Mother,' he said. 'She's

always wanted goldfish.'

Just then a bell rang loudly. 'Oh, what a pity! It's time to go,' said Moon-Face, getting up. 'They turn you out of the Land of Treats every evening, you know. No one is allowed to stay here for the night. It's too magic. Come on, we must go!'

Rather sadly they went to the hole in the cloud, with a crowd of other visitors. They went down to Moon-Face's, and there Connie said goodbye.

'I'm going home tomorrow,' she said, 'but I have had a wonderful time, I really have. Goodbye, Moon-Face, and thank you for rescuing me from the ladder-that-has-no-top. Goodbye, Watzisname, I hope you remember your real name some time. Goodbye, dear Silky, it has been lovely to know you. Goodbye, Saucepan! I'm sorry you thought I was a nasty little girl.'

Saucepan actually heard what she said. 'Oh, you're much nicer now,' he said, 'much, much nicer. Come back again. You may get nicer still then!'

'Goodbye everyone in the Faraway Tree!' said Connie.

They all went down the Tree. Connie said goodbye to the little red squirrel. 'You're the best little squirrel I ever knew! Goodbye!' she said.

They went through the Enchanted Wood, and the trees whispered to Connie. 'Wisha, wisha, wisha!'

'They're wishing me goodbye,' said Connie. 'Oh Joe, Beth, Frannie, how lucky you are to live near the Enchanted Wood, and to be able to go up the Faraway Tree whenever you like. I wish I did too!'

So do I, don't you?

The End

The Enchanted Wood

*'I feel as if there are adventures about,' said
Joe. 'Come on!'*

When Joe, Beth and Frannie move to the
country, they discover they are living next to
the mysterious Enchanted Wood. And deep in
the wood is the oldest and most magical tree
in the world—the Faraway Tree!

The children soon meet Silky the fairy,
friendly Moon-face, the deaf old Saucepan
Man and many other enchanting little folk.
Join them on their exciting adventures as they
visit the amazing lands at the top of the
Faraway Tree.

The first book in Enid Blyton's classic
Faraway Tree series.

The Magic Faraway Tree

'The Enchanted Wood!' said Beth softly. 'What marvellous adventures we have had there.'

Deep in the Enchanted Wood grows the Faraway Tree—the oldest, most magical tree in the world. Follow the adventures of Joe, Beth, Frannie and their cousin Rick, as they visit the many exciting lands at the top of the Tree.

Meet their enchanting friends, Silky the fairy, friendly Moon-face, the funny, deaf old Saucepan Man, grumpy Watzisname, Dame Washalot and a host of other magical characters.

The second book in Enid Blyton's classic Faraway Tree series.